*To Leslie,
Thank you for
always being there
when I need you.
Love you always!
Susan*

FAITH OF A CHILD

By

Susan Lamar Blish

This book is a work of fiction. Places, events, and situations in this story are purely fictional. Any resemblance to actual persons, living or dead, is coincidental.

© 2002 by Susan Lamar Blish. All rights reserved.

No part of this book may be reproduced, stored in a retrieval system, or transmitted by any means, electronic, mechanical, photocopying, recording, or otherwise, without written permission from the author.

ISBN: 1-4033-5390-5 (e-book)
ISBN: 1-4033-5391-3 (Paperback)
ISBN: 1-4033-5392-1 (Dustjacket)

Library of Congress Control Number: 2002093275

This book is printed on acid free paper.

Printed in the United States of America
Bloomington, IN

1st Books - rev. 08/19/02

This book is dedicated to

The Glory of

God the Father

The Ancient of Days

For the Dream

I would like to thank

The following for their help

And non-stop faith in my ability:

Spryte for those long nights of re-reading

Gentle criticism and spelling corrections

My mother who told me to get to it

And Leslie for the push because

She wanted to know the rest.

iv

TABLE OF CONTENTS

INTRODUCTION vii
THE ROOM 2
THE FAITH OF A CHILD 19
THE TWO MEN 37
THE MIST 46
THE VEIL 55
REDEMPTION   PART I 63
THE DEMONS 68
REDEMPTION   PART II 78
REDEMPTION   PART III 87
THE CHALLENGE 99
THE CHOICE 107

vi

INTRODUCTION

My name is Susan. I'm a basic in most of my dealings type of person. I have bottled blonde hair and green eyes. I'm about 5'4" and a bit over weight.

I was born January 6, 1956, in Tacoma, Washington. My birthday is celebrated on a religious holiday known as Epiphany.

As an adult, I looked up the word Epiphany and discovered that it means,

"Revelation of Jesus as the Christ celebrated January 6th."

Nice day to celebrate a birthday don't you agree?

My life is generally considered normal by most any measure taken. I spent a good deal of my youth in Church, here in Tacoma. It wasn't an option. Our family attended The Salvation Army Church, a Methodist Based Doctrine and unless you were dead, you were going.

When I reached adulthood and married, my husband and I attended services on a semi-regular basis. We did what a lot of young people seem to do, attend because it was expected, not because we really wanted to be there, and over time, once our children had been Dedicated, we stopped attending.

I thought that I had a great relationship with God, and understood what "having a personal relationship with Jesus" meant. I had asked and been accepted as a member of the church, wore the Uniform of a Senior Soldier, attended Friday night youth meeting, and each year attended the Youth Conference sponsored by the Church. I'd bow my head and pray along with the rest but mostly just didn't talk with God. I attended Sunday regular church meetings, gave money when I had it and watched the few Christian movies that were out at the time. I read "Inspirational" Books, and memorized certain Bible passages and verses; I even went forward several times to the altar and had people pray for me. I did all the things that I thought you were supposed to do in order to be a good Christian. However, I did not do two things that I should have. One, *ask* and *accept* God's forgiveness and entrance into my heart and life along with His will, and secondly, fully read and study the Bible, the Word of God. Oh I was great at asking, but it was the acceptance, the allowing of God to remove those blotches from my heart that kept me from Him. That was something all together different. I had asked often enough, but never really believed that I, with *my* past, could be forgiven. I felt as long as I remembered what those things were, that God also would remember them.

I was great at Lip Service. I didn't *really* want to admit to any one that I never fully felt forgiven or that I just didn't "get it."

I'd look at the faces of some people that I knew had that special walk with God. They had such a look of bliss; a look that said they were at peace, and I longed for those same feelings. I wanted to share in that look of rapture, understanding and love. I'd ask them often enough, what they had done, and they would very often offer

viii

to pray for or with me right there on the spot. I'd always shy away from them while thinking to myself, "Are they serious?" Right here in front of every one? How embarrassing!" After a period of time, I stopped asking God for anything. I walked away. From the church, from those eyes that I felt knew me to my core but most of all, from God, his love and his protection.

I figured that I had a lot of time before the so called "second coming" would take place. I was young and felt I was immortal, that death or the end of the world would not come for a very long time. I thank God each day that He has not come before now.

Now at this writing and time in my life it seems every one of my views, my faith and I believe my life has all changed and come into full focus with a dream.

I am now within a week's time of being 46-years-old. I have relative good health and not usually one to give into Delusions of Grandeur. I've never thought of myself as special in any way.

I was awakened one morning in December 2001, knowing immediately that I had through the course of the night, received a message or vision of enlightenment.

I do not think of myself as divinely blessed. Yet, I cannot help but think that God has chosen me for perhaps this one thing. I must follow my thinking and belief that God can and will do as he chooses and remember that He is all knowing, all loving, and all forgiving. God is the Master that will never give us more than we can deal with at any time. He will never set us up for failure. It is His desire that we reach out for Him.

I have never been one to think for a moment that I know the mind of God. I do believe the Bible was given to man through the inspiration of God, and it states:

".... I will pour out my spirit on all people. Your sons and daughters will prophesy, your old men will dream dreams, your young men will see visions. Even on my servants, both the men and the women, I will pour out my spirit in those days. (NIV Joel 2:28-29)"

I have no idea why I have had this dream, but I feel pressed to put it to paper. It is my hope that the readers will be able to grow in their love of God, and approach their faith with a new understanding of His will and direction. We need to understand that God will allow some things in our life. It is His desire that in time of sorrow and grief, just as in times of great joy, that we will come to Him, as his children and fully accept our part as his creation. He is always there, waiting to infuse us with pure love, and joy.

The dream did not wake me from my sleep as so many in the past have done. It was my roommate that woke me and she seemed concerned because I was talking in my sleep, not something that I am prone to do.

I was not totally coherent and seemed to be talking in what she described as gibberish. As I fully woke, the full force of the dream became very clear to me. It did, for some time upset me, and cause me great pain and tears when I tried to recount it. It also gave me a renewed hope that God is always with us, that we are His children deeply loved and cherished. It showed me a new understanding of what true, pure love is, and why God created us.

With God as my Guide, Lord and Savior, I hope to recount as clearly as I can, my interpretation and understanding of that dream.

Faith of a Child

CHAPTER 1

…Then Joseph said to them

"Do not interpretations belong to God?

Tell me your dreams…" (NIV Genesis 40:8)

Susan Lamar Blish

The Room

There, I was finished with my email. I sat back in my chair and looked at the time. Picking up my marker, I looked at the calendar. December 28th, 2001. I marked another day off and sighed. Just three more days and this year would be over. I wondered to myself "Have I learned any new lessons this year?" It had not been a great year for me, but then, my life was not that different from most people. I reminded myself that life is not always a bed of roses, but I was just a tad bit tired of nothing but thorns. I sighed again as I reflected back on the day. I wondered if I was ever going to get a new job.

My day had started out uneventful, as most of my days had been over the past few months. My life was pretty basic with seldom anything new or unusual happening. I have to honestly say that I, like most people stick to a very basic routine in my life. I am not one of those people that loved or craved a lot of excitement. The holidays were in full swing with Christmas just past.

I was not overly involved with the Christmas Cheer this year as the money was tight. I'd recently lost my job as a Billing Specialist for a medical billing company. Every penny counted.

As the evening wore on, I was slightly depressed, and decided to call it a day and head off to bed at about 11:00 P.M. Little did I know that as I went to bed, it would be a night that I would never forget.

Faith of a Child

The New Year loomed on the horizon with all of the dreams of a better year. Getting ready for bed, I was contemplating the customary setting of resolutions I felt would insure a superior coming year.

I got into bed and set my alarm to go off at 7:30 A.M., a time that I felt was reasonable, seeing that the next day was Saturday. I knew at that time of the morning I would not *really* be willing to get up. Like most people that I knew, I would hit the snooze button a few times before eventually getting up and starting my day.

I pulled the heavy blankets up over my shoulders and snuggled under the heavy quilts and closed my eyes. I tried to relax as much as I could, and, after praying, a habit I had recently started, I regulated my breathing and started to drift off to sleep.

I heard something.

I knew that I had locked the doors before coming to bed. The apartment was dark and as I strained to single out the sound, I could hear my roommate, who had gone to bed a bit before me, quietly snoring, so I knew it wasn't her. "It had to be the cats playing," I thought to myself. I have two cats, Rusty who believes himself to be"the man about town" of the cat world and weighs in at a rousting 26 pounds of pure black cat attitude just looking for a place to happen, and Scampi who thinks that "SHE" is in charge of all the midnight entertainment and games of the local kitty club chapter in Pierce County. I thought to myself, "If they keep it up, I'll deal with it then".

Susan Lamar Blish

I was used to a certain amount of noise at night. Scampi was notorious for starting to play what we call "cup hockey". A game that involved knocking anything that she felt was fair game onto the floor and bating it around for as long as she felt she could, with me being the goal at one end of the apartment and the couch in the living room being the other goal. She would start as soon as she could roust Rusty from his sleep after the lights had gone out. She had also recently taken to opening the cupboard doors at night and letting them bang closed, I assumed in an effort to engage me in a game of chase.

I heard it again.

Thinking to myself, "I'll kill them, I am too tired to deal with this tonight," I tossed back the covers, and with an unhappy groan, got out of bed and reached for the light switch. I turned on the light and when I blinked from the brightness of it, I found myself standing in a grayish area, an enclave of sorts. I said out loud, "**Now this is festive**". I looked back at where my bed should have been and there was nothing there but the huge expansion of a room.

"That's odd," I thought to myself, "I don't remember the alarm going off". I knew that I had gone to bed, and that fuzzy feeling you have when the alarm wakes you from a deep sleep was not there. Feeling a bit misplaced and very uncomfortable in my new surroundings I quickly looked to the left and right, trying to figure out just where I was and what had happened.

4

Faith of a Child

I pinched myself and felt the pain that signals that I was in fact awake and not sleeping. I checked the next morning, and there was indeed a bruise where I had pinched myself.

Something struck a cord deep with in me, telling me this was all wrong.

As my eyes adjusted to the light of the room, I found that there were other people there with me. It was very clear by the look on their faces that they too had just materialized and like myself, found that they were standing in strange surroundings. In the blink of an eye, a moment of time, I was fully awake, and my senses were in overdrive.

As my confusion at the sudden arrival dissipated a bit, I tried to remember some of the most basic emergency training I had learned over the years. Survival mode was kicking in full tilt, and after the initial checklist of hands and feet, what was working what was not; I realized that I needed to find an exit. I turned my head around to look in vain and tried to locate one. I knew that I could judge the distance to the exit and calculate how long it would take me to get out of this place, but I was not able to locate one. I could not gain my bearings and was beginning to feel the icy grip of something unsettling. As the grip of fear settled on me, my pulse quickened a bit. I began to feel slightly panicked. My hands felt cold and clammy and I was shaking, almost chilled with the feelings of it all. I did not like this one bit.

As I looked around at my surroundings wide eyed, I wondered,

Susan Lamar Blish

"Who are all of these people, and where did they all come from?"

"Do I know these people from some place?"

"Why are we all here?"

"Who brought us here?"

I began to shout out to anyone that might hear," **What's going on?!"**

With no answer or reply to my shouts I tried to calm down slightly. Nothing suggested to me that we were in any danger so I began to look around a bit more boldly. I wondered just how many people were here with me. I tried several times, but was not able to count the number of people. I even stood on my toes to look as far as I could, and was amazed, for they were as far as the eye could see and became a blur into the distance. Some were very small children, not more than perhaps two or three, and others seemed to be exceedingly old as if they had lived to be over 100. As I strained and looked, it appeared that every race and nationality was represented in all of the age brackets. Terror struck me as I asked myself, "Is this the final judgment?"

I took a deep breath in an attempt to shake off the feelings of dread that seemed to come with the suddenness of my arrival. As I attempted to relax a bit, I first turned my head then my body and looked around. I got a closer view of the people that surrounded me. I saw hundreds of children and what could only be described as "The look of Innocence" you see when children are sleeping. It

Faith of a Child

almost looked as if they had a small glow about them. It was brightly lit on all of their faces. I saw as well, some of the adults had that same look. However, on faces of people that were closest to me, I saw looks that I knew must have been showing on my own, amazement, confusion, shock, and fear. All of them were showing in one way or another.

As I stood there, I had that uneasiness again, feelings of alarm that come from the unknown. I just couldn't shake that sensation. I almost felt as if something was crawling on my skin. Something was wrong, so very, very wrong. It was just a twinge; something gripping me in the pit of my stomach, but it was there. I started to feel a bit lightheaded as the panic settled over me.

I was starting to convince myself that this was in fact a dream, an incredibly bad dream. "Susan", I thought, "You have got to wake up!"

As the suddenness of my arrival there eased away, I became yet more aware of my surroundings.

As I looked around a bit more I wondered again, "What is this place?' 'This really doesn't feel like one of my dreams."

Again, I felt that twinge. It was a bit stronger and *"closer?"* "Whatever it is", I thought, "I don't think I want to be on the welcoming committee.

Again I looked for an exit, with the same results.

Looking around I began to focus more on the area as a whole. I thought to myself, "Wow, this place is huge!" In all of my memory, I

Susan Lamar Blish

can not remember any thing coming close to the size of the space that I was in. I felt **so0o0o** small and almost lost in the magnitude of it.

It was an enormous place, one that we would commonly call a room, nonetheless, it was larger by far than any stadium or building that I had ever seen. From the looks of it, it was able to hold thousands upon thousands of people. It had no walls that could be seen or sensed. Even after standing on my toes, I did not feel that into the distance, walls existed. There was a floor and what appeared to be a ceiling of the same color, creating without seam the whole area. The color was luminous in shade, more than just white, and the area was well lit. I had no problems seeing everyone and everything, and there were no shadows cast, even from the people! I have no idea where the light came from, as there were no fixtures that I could see. The area "felt" bright with light, not the blinding light you sometimes see or feel in larger rooms such as an auditorium or arena. No, **This** was not a normal light. It was soft in color and had a texture if that is possible. I felt the light reverberate through me as much as I saw it.

As I stood there, one area of the room, I guessed it to be the center of my area, got brighter, and more intense. However, as bright as it was, it appeared to be diffused by some means, softening, as it got brighter. As I tried to register the feeling of the light, it almost reminded me of a light that had a white plastic cover over it. As I looked at the light, it was warm and inviting, as if it was

Faith of a Child

calling me. I almost felt as if it had a voice. I tried to focus on the light, but soon my attention drifted to other areas of the room.

I tried to take in all of the notable facts of the room, reminding myself that in the past, talking with some of my friends about dreams and things, we often compared notes to see if we could figure out as a group what the dreams had meant. This, I was sure; they would find intriguing and we would spend a great many hours discussing to the tiniest detail, what it all meant. I was very sure that they would call the area many things, the zone, a chamber, or perhaps the gray area.

We as a group had discussed every thing from little green men, the big bang theory, evolution, and all the major religions. We often discussed what we felt would be the best religion by taking a bit here and there creating a new world order. We had also discussed how we arrived here on earth and what the meaning of life was.

I was reasonably sure with my eclectic friends, that a few would claim to have been in this same space themselves, and as usual, recounting what they had seen, as one of mist or haze. Over the years, we had often discussed rooms that we had visited while in the dream state. When discussing being in rooms and such, many had stated the ability to see and feel, yet, for no known reason, they had always felt closed in.

This was not that feeling. I don't know why, but I knew this was going to be different. I wondered while standing there, if my friends would believe me when I told them about THIS room.

Susan Lamar Blish

A few days after this experience, I did share portions of my vision with them, and in doing so; I could sense the fear they felt. This was out of character for most of them. This time, most of them claimed a total lack of understanding as to any meaning at all, and yet, I could see something on their faces. I knew that they were experiencing in a way new to them, a united apprehension as if they almost remembered being there themselves. I could see it in their eyes and hear it in their voices when they tried to ask me questions or while we were discussing the dream and its meanings. Most denied they were there, something that was totally out of character for a good number of the friends that I had.

I've often wondered in the past about people who tell me "I've had that same dream!" Some educators have said it is mass hypnosis or hysteria that causes this. I no longer believe that this is the case. I now understand that a good portion of the population can and often do share what appears to be the same dream or at the very least, portions of an identicalness while in the dream state. Are these from God? I don't know. What I do know is that this dream was different and it was something that I prayed no one else had to see or feel.

Several people were talking with each other as if trying to see if anyone knew where we were, and what had happened. "Well" I said to myself, "At least we can talk to each other".

I asked myself, and heard others ask while standing there taking in the surroundings,

Faith of a Child

"Where was this place?"

"How did I get here?"

"Is this from God?"

"Is this just a bad dream?"

"Didn't God send dreams to those in the Old Testament to teach them?"

"Is this what I was going thru?"

"Was God testing me, testing my faith?"

""Is this the final judgment?"

My mind wondered a bit and I wondered about the other people there. I knew many of them, if not by name, then by face. Conversely, there were countless that I didn't recognize, but felt that I somehow knew.

Here in the northwest, we are blessed to have a large population of deer, and very often a deer or group of deer will be feeding along the highways not noticing how close they may be to the street. Unfortunately, at night, one will step out onto the main road and be blinded by the lights of an oncoming car. They simply stand there, not able to move. It is known as the "deer in the headlights look." It say's "I'm afraid, but don't know why." That's the look that I saw on the faces of the people around me. Most of those close to me had the same look of confusion and panic that I shared with them.

At least I had a confirmation that others were feeling what I was and I was not alone in my thoughts.

Susan Lamar Blish

I tried to remain calm and keep my wits about me, yet I heard the sound of my heart beating in my ears and I shook with uncontrollable fear.

There was not much movement from the people in the room, and I, like many of the others there with me, just stood in the same place they had appeared. Some were looking around trying to take in what had just happened to them. I wondered if they had arrived the same way that I had.

I heard, a quiet hum of conversation in the room that helped with the unsettling feelings I was having. You would expect with that number of people, to have a clamor so loud that you would not be able to hear yourself think, yet, it was the **lack** of noise that sent new dread into me. I knew from the look of the others around me, I was not alone in thinking this.

I heard a soft voice say,*" You must have the faith of a child."* I looked around to see where the voice had come from, but was not able to see any one looking at me, and wondered if I was hearing things as well.

Each of us stood in what was about a 4-foot square. The floor was well lit and reminded me of the 1970's disco style floor as each section the person was standing on was lit and there was a small divider separating each block of light. The floor felt solid under my feet and I noticed that I was not wearing any type of shoes or socks. I looked at other people's feet and no one had on any type of foot wear that I could see. I wondered why.

Faith of a Child

The floor was not cold, but again I was reminded of iciness without being chilly.

There was that tingle again. My skin felt like it was charged with electricity, and the hair on my arms was standing up. I felt that same deep winter type of freezing that almost burns your skin. It was as if someone or something was breathing that coldness onto my neck and down my back. I twisted my body around a bit to see what was behind me, and shivered with the thought of it, but nothing was there.

With no warning, I was drawn back to reality. Did something move? YES. I saw a movement out of the corner of my eye. It was a shimmer of sorts. The room its self seemed to have a mind or soul of its own. It appeared to me, this place we were in, had breath and was **alive**.

I asked myself, "What is the reason we are all here?"

"Why did I see an unbridled fear in the eyes of some and a total serenity in the face of others?"

I just didn't understand and had a very hard time taking all of this in.

I still had questions.

"Had I died?"

"Had we been kidnapped?"

My mind raced with panic as I questioned every thing that was happening.

Susan Lamar Blish

Something told me that whatever was going to happen would happen soon, and I knew that what ever it was, I wasn't going to like it.

I had the impression of something within this area. Cold. Distance. Anger. Hate. Malice. Every emotion at once and I felt it was about to consume me. However, the one that hit the hardest was the *bitterness*. The odd thing was, it was without the actual physical feeling of "a person."

I remember not actually "seeing" anything in the physical sense. Nothing I could see would give me that feeling, yet the identity of substance or understanding was there. I felt my emotions with such a new intensity that I wondered if I had ever felt them before.

Then, suddenly, I felt the icy grip that surrounds your heart and makes it hard to breathe or think... Terror. That deep seeded feeling when you're all alone on a dark night. You **think** you hear voices, or footsteps behind you. You **KNOW** something is there, nonetheless, when you turn your head to look, nothing **is** there. It's instinctive. You just can't shake that feeling no matter what you do. Even in the confines of your own car or home you're not sure you're safe. It was that fear of the unknown. And it was getting worse with each passing moment.

As I wondered at all I was seeing and feeling a new realization hit me. This was not like the usual surreal feelings or view normally held in the dream state. NoOoOo... **This** was different. I didn't know how, but I had transcended every thing that I know about nighttime

Faith of a Child

visions, and this was nothing like that. I felt my heart beating faster and faster as I realized with a renewed horror that this was real. **THIS WAS REAL!**

As I took in the full shock of being in this strange place, panic took hold of me, and all I could think was "I have to get out of here". I wanted to run, but did not have the ability to move. Something held me fast to my block of light.

In my panicked state I asked myself, "If I called on God, would He answer?, If I did call what would He do?, Did I really know how to call on God?, If I called on God, and He didn't answer, what would I do then?"

I wanted to run and hide, but I wasn't sure from what.

I heard the voice again say,

"You are a child of God, have faith."

I have always thought that I had been able to control my emotional response to things. Somehow this was all too new for me to grasp and I felt doubt. It was present in my thoughts and I was questioning every ounce of faith I once had, and in my heart and soul, I felt as if my faith was being attacked and put to the test. I soon discovered that this was exactly, what was happening.

I did not know or understand how this strange and frightening occurrence had come about, but I knew that God was allowing this. I noticed once again the shimmer I had seen earlier and I focused on it for a moment. It almost became solid but was more of a mist. I heard a deep voice within the mist said:

Susan Lamar Blish

"TRUST GOD WITHOUT A DOUBT OR YOU WILL DIE."

After hearing this, the mist dissolved again. Or maybe it simply wasn't there to start with. "I'm loosing my mind," I thought.

I have no idea where the voice came from or if it had actually been real. Instinct told me that it was real. The statement that death would be final, and that there would be no chance for redemption, that was real too. What ever this was, I knew that I, and every other person who had been brought there, had to face this, and our existence was on the line. My life, my faith, my very being would never again remain the same.

I tried to calm myself a bit and as I looked around, noticed that every one was dressed alike. We were all wearing what looked to be long white robes. They were simple in design, with no addition of color or pattern and were made of a simple linen or cotton like material yet they draped like silky breezy gossamer and moved freely.

We had a simple sash around our waist that was made of the same material to hold the robe in place. There was an opening at the neck that came to a small "v" shape that had no closure and they appeared to simply drape over the body. The robes all had long sleeves. It was plain that the robe was made just for the person who was wearing it, as the fit was perfect in length and width. The clothing was enough to keep out the cold if the room had been cold.

Faith of a Child

In a brief instant, a moment of time that seemed endless, I felt a new and awesome emotion resonate through me causing me to shake uncontrollably. As soon as it passed I asked myself, "Who were all of these people and why we were all here?"

The horrendous answer came soon enough.

Susan Lamar Blish

CHAPTER 2

"But Jesus called the children to him and said,
"Let the little children come to me, and do not hinder them,
For the kingdom of God belongs to such as these.
I tell you the truth, anyone who will not receive the kingdom
Of God like a little child will never enter it."
(NIV Luke 18:16-17)

THE FAITH OF A CHILD

I stood there in shock, looking around the room trying to take in all that had happened, and I thought to myself, "What did the voice mean when it said, you must have the faith of a child? Who was behind that voice and where was it coming from? Why did the voice sound familiar? Was it someone that I knew?"

I tried to wake up again.

I was frightened as I stood there. Nothing was as it should have been. I *knew* I should have been in bed sleeping; the alarm had not gone off, yet I knew that I was not dreaming. Or was I? Was this just a bad dream? Something told me I was no longer in my bed. What ever this was, it was no dream.

I tried to shake off the strange feelings I was having. I felt like I was on a roller coaster. I don't like roller coasters. They terrify me. I get shaky when I am around them. I know that a lot of people love the thrill of them, but I am one of those that actually get sick to my stomach and scream when I am on one. I felt like I was on an E ticket ride and I wanted off!

As I was trying to get a grip on my emotions, I felt a strange calm in the room. It was a breather of sorts. I sighed and for a moment felt relaxed.

As I settled again into the feelings of the room, I looked around a bit more. There seemed to be some of the adults that were not affected by the whole ordeal. "Why?" I asked myself. "What made them so special?" I wanted to know how they could stand there and

Susan Lamar Blish

smile. Then I noticed that they had that same glow about them that I had seen on the children earlier.

Something told me that they knew what was going on and they were almost expecting it. I wanted desperately to run to them and ask them if they knew what was happening, but I could not move outside of my little box. Even though there were no walls to hold me there, I was somehow locked within my square of light.

I shrugged as I looked at them. "Maybe they are angels," I thought. I believed in angels as a child and had always thought they were sent to protect us. I didn't really believe that these people were angels, however, in this strange place nothing else was making a lot of sense, and if it gave me some comfort in thinking that they were, why not?

I turned away from the rest of the room and kind of settled into a semi-sitting position trying to come to terms with everything that I was seeing and hearing. As I rocked back on my heels, I felt like I was beginning to loose what little control I had of my mind.

As I sat there with my knees to my chin, I saw my mother on my right. I had no idea where she had come from. I had not noticed her before. I hoped that she had been brought here to help me. As I looked at her, she was still struggling with the arrival and I did not try and speak to her.

As I sat in my block of light, even though it gave me assurance, I felt trapped here. No matter how I looked at things, I didn't see

Faith of a Child

any way out. I knew that I would have to stay here until whatever was going to happen, had fully transpired. I sighed in my frustration.

I tried to focus on what I was feeling. I wondered, "Could I define just one emotion?" They kept coming at me so fast it was hard to spotlight just one. The emotional upheaval was getting harder and harder to deal with. My feelings went from one end of the spectrum to the other. Just when I thought I had experienced all of them, a new emotion arrived.

With out warning I felt it. Hate. I felt all the trappings that come with it and my mind raced with the emotion. I tried to shake it off. "Where did this one come from?" I wondered. How could someone or something that I could not see, bring about all of this?" I began to cry again.

The force of it hit me like a ton of bricks. This was one emotion that I had been told could really take me away from God. My mother used to tell me that I didn't really hate any one. She would say, "That emotion is just too strong, and maybe it's just a deep dislike".

I couldn't *really* remember hating anyone my whole life. Then it dawned on me. There was **one**. I remember hating with such intensity that nothing else felt like it, only one person as I grew up. I used to stay awake at night and plan on how I would take this persons life. "Yes", I thought as I reflected back on it, I would have actually killed this person had I had the chance. It had been this person that was responsible for taking my childhood away from me.

Susan Lamar Blish

As I was pondering that one moment in my life, I saw that shimmer of the mist again and as the mist took on a shape I could clearly see it was a movie of sorts. The scene unfolded before me, and I saw a young child, a little girl of about four, running and laughing. She was running down what appeared to be a sidewalk, away from a house. I noticed that the small green house was old and not well kept, and was set off the road. It had a broken down small white picket fence that went across the front yard and long sidewalk that had a rose trellis at the end of it. As I looked further, I saw that the sky was blue with just a few light puffy clouds and the air smelled sweet with the scent of a spring day. The rose arbor at the end of the sidewalk seemed to be the little girl's goal and she ran laughing and shrieking with abandon.

I thought to myself "The house looked familiar". As I watched, I could not place in my memory where I had known it, but I knew that I had been there before. Then the understanding of the little girl struck me. I gasped! It was, me, as a little girl, and I was beginning to remember something from my past. I smiled softly to myself, remembering how much fun that day was.

I was playing with my make believe friend. To me she was very real! I could actually see her and talk with her and she was always there when I needed her. Oh, she was so full of encouragement and love! I wanted to be just like her when I grew up. She knew how to hug better than anyone. At that time, my mother was

Faith of a Child

struggling to make it as a single parent, and was not able to really show her own children love.

I asked myself, "What was her name"? "Judy", I suddenly remembered. Her name was Judy! She was mine alone, no one else could see her and she was my guardian angel.

I watched and remembered; we were playing she reminded me that I could not go past the rose trellis into the street. She was teaching me how to fly. She told me that I had to flap my arms really hard and then, just before the end of the sidewalk, I would be able to jump out of my body and fly with her. Oh how I remembered! She showed me so many things. She showed me that morning glory flowers smelled really good first thing in the morning when the dew was still on them and that caterpillars do change into beautiful butterflies, and that baby kittens were soft and full of love. She taught me that if you put a dandelion flower under your chin, you could see yellow.

Many children have playmates that they create. Mine was Judy, and I loved her. I smiled with the love that I felt at that moment in time, and with out realizing it, I allowed a tear to fall.

I heard a small whisper ask,

"Child of God, why do you weep"?

I was not aware that I had started to cry for the child of so long ago, the one that had the ability to believe in angels and in a loving God that would never leave me. I angrily wiped the tear away and growled as I said, "I had to grow up and take responsibilities and I

Susan Lamar Blish

had no choice. That child, that innocence is dead and long gone". I denied that it ever truly existed.

I don't know when I stopped believing in angels and the joy that they had brought into my life. I don't know when I stopped having the faith of a child, but I do know that I never talked with my children about those times. Like most adults, I had forgotten by then about my playmate.

When I had children of my own, I asked my mother if I had any make believe friends or playmates. She said that she "thought" I had one, but honestly couldn't remember. It seemed strange now, that I could remember Judy telling me that as long as I had faith, I could do anything, and that God, had assigned her to me. She, like God would always love me and was always with me. Why had I forgotten? I just didn't know.

I stood there lost in the memory of my childhood, trying to remember that quiet time in my life.

I settled back into a semi-sitting position and as I sat there, I heard a voice from my past that sent chills through me, the words that seared the mind, heart and soul of a child *"If you tell, I'll be in trouble, and you don't want me to be in trouble do you?"*

I looked around trying to see if he was really there or if it was the mist talking to me. I looked at the mist but it was not moving. The voice, that man, had been the person that had taken my innocence. I felt the same volume of hate that I had years ago when it had all happened.

Faith of a Child

I was brought back to reality when the mist moved again. I stood up to watch what it had to show me. It was showing more of my childhood. I looked at my mom and was about to ask her a question when I stopped. Either she did not notice my looking at her or did not see what I was seeing. I saw tears running down her face. I wanted to comfort her and when I started to ask her what was wrong, the mist shifted, and I just had to look at it. I wailed, "I don't want to see this!" and I tried to turn away from the scene before me, but I couldn't. I did not want to face more of my childhood memories. My childhood was one that no person wants to remember, and I could not believe I was seeing this!

I stood mute for a moment, in a state of shock. I watched the mist, and I was seeing and remembering the pain of the first one, that first time as a young girl of five, when I was molested. I saw and heard my cousin telling me that if it hurt, he would stop, and he promised me that he would take me for a ride on the go-carts if I were very good, but that this was our little secret. He made me promise not to tell anyone because he might get into trouble, and then he said, *"No one will believe you because you're a child"*. And there was the blood again, and I felt the pain sear through my mind and body once again as he penetrated me, just as he had so many years ago.

The tears came in rivers as I stood there in my pain and humiliation. I knew that no matter what, I was just as guilty as I stood there, as I had been as a child of five on the day that it

25

Susan Lamar Blish

happened. I hung my head in shame and let the guilt flood over me. I knew too, that just as they could see the guilt all over me as a child, the people around me could see it now.

I knew that this was not the end of the projection and I was right.

Just as the pain was more than I could bear, the scene blurred a bit, and almost seemed to seep away. I took a deep breath, and then before I had the chance to recoup my emotions, once again a new projection was there. It was before my eyes, the time when I was 13 and my mother's man-friend told me that it was his job to teach me about the men that would come into my life and what being a woman was about. Later that night, after it was over, I just knew that my mother could see the guilt I felt each time she looked at me. I felt it now, again, as deeply as that day that seemed like one hundred years ago. The day that I was forever changed. I was no longer a little girl. I was now, and forever more guilty. And I knew it showed.

I turned away from my mother, even though she was not looking at me, I knew she would be able to see "THAT LOOK" of guilt again all over me.

I watched the mist and remembered that I felt dirty for years after that, never again embracing the clean that comes from those that are untouched.

I was so naïve at that time in my life. I believed that when someone said that they loved you, they were telling the truth. It was not long after that when I learned that is not always the case. Lots

Faith of a Child

of people told me that I was somehow different. I thought they all could tell that I was unclean. No one knew the full truth for years. I managed to keep that part of myself, secret.

I changed a lot after that second time. I was 14 and very aware of my budding sexuality. I saw within the mist the boy's that lived across the street, and how they used to tap on my bedroom window and invite me out into the night. It wasn't long before the inevitable happened. I was quietly sent away for the birth of a little boy. I was an embarrassment to my family. My shame, and my guilt were more than I could bear at the time and I felt that shame and guilt as keenly as the day it all happened.

I remember praying to God everyday that he would save me and make all of the pain go away. I wanted him to make me clean again. I prayed that all of this was nothing more than a bad dream.

I never felt forgiven. I reasoned "If I remembered, then I knew that God too would remember and hold it against me".

I used to change my name from time to time. Just slight variations of my own name. At times in my life, as now, I insisted on being called Susan. She was the one that I wanted to be. I always felt strong, efficient, levelheaded and in control. I feared no one. I had become the user. Other times, I went by Sue, that little girl type of demeanor that was full of love and innocence, who could laugh with abandon and loved life. As Sue, I attempted to recapture the feelings of yesterday that I had lost, with all the hopes of a child. Eventually, I adopted Saundra. She was streetwise and used every

27

Susan Lamar Blish

one she could as often as she could. She had the reputation of someone that would start a fight if she thought it would serve her purpose. No one dared cross her.

NO, I was not a split personality. Not by a long shot. But I did feel different at times, and the subtle name change, was my way of rebelling.

As I remembered all of the torture a child goes through, the pain was refreshed and I felt it as intensely as I did the day that it happened. I didn't think I could keep crying like this. I was so wrong.

Why show this, my being molested, my pain and the humiliation of it, the embarrassment of it all? I wept. Why force me to see this when I had worked so hard to forget it?

I heard a new soft and loving voice within the mist say, *"You had the faith of a child, can you believe as one again?"*

"No way", I thought to myself. I raised my arm and pointed to the scene before me. I shouted *"My faith left me when I was that child, at the same time my innocence was taken from me!"*

I was angry! And that anger burned inside of me like a non-quenchable fire. I felt all of the anger and all of the hate well up in me like a spring, and I knew it would be a long time before those feelings left me again.

The mist shifted, and I felt something brush my arm. I turned my head to see what had touched me but all I saw was empty space and I heard a deep evil low laugh, and a spiteful voice say,

"You had innocence and now you're guilty."

I turned to the sound and **DEMANDED,** *"WHO SAID THAT?!"*

The voice kindled in my heart a new hatred and anger, and sent a new round of cold chills through me. I felt the hate building inside of me. I didn't care any more about who I hurt, or why. I would get even with any one and every one that had ever hurt me!! I would hunt down every one that had ever been the cause of my pain and they would suffer as I was suffering now! They didn't know what I was capable of doing and it didn't matter any more who knew it or who was the target of my emotion. **Someone was going to pay!**

As I was delighting in my new plan, I heard that voice again. This time it was laughing, with a maniacal glee.

The mist moved again and I was drawn to it, away from that voice. I turned to watch this new scene unfold. It was now showing me a time when in elementary school, I was the target of the other kids. They went out of their way to make fun of me and ridicule me, and I began to feel the tears well up in my eyes once again.

I started to scream at the mist, "stop it, Stop It, STOP IT!" I was out of control with my emotions. I could not deal any more with the upheaval I was experiencing and felt exhausted by the enormity of it. I was suicidal in my thoughts and wanted to lie down and die.

"NO MORE", I pleaded. "I CAN'T TAKE ANY MORE". I tried again to stop the tears. It was useless. I was not even sure what I was crying about any more. Maybe it was the pain of being forced

Susan Lamar Blish

to remember all of this again, to see and feel once again the little girl lost in someone else's desire.

How could you go from hearing the cats play in the dark to just blinking and being here? Nothing made any sense.

This roller coaster had to stop! My emotions keep changing. One minute I was calm and thinking rationally looking at things from a survivor's view and then with no warning I was terrified and seeing and feeling all the pain of a horrible childhood. I actually got to the point that I didn't care about what would happen next. I felt angry, lost and confused and currently, I was a dead person inside. I didn't want to think any more. I pleaded with God, "Just let me die".

As I saw it, there was no real direction or target for my feelings. I needed someone to blame for all of this. I wanted to know who was causing all of this to happen and why. There was no one that I could directly point to which would cause any of this. Oh sure, the mist was showing me things I didn't want to see, and relive, but outside of that, I had no one to point at that would be the cause for my feelings and all I could do was cry. I told myself, "I just didn't care any more."

As that thought crossed my mind, I felt a calming flood over me and I struggled to relax for a moment. It felt like a lifeline to me. As I sighed at the reprieve, I wondered, "What was going to happen next?" As I thought about it, suddenly…there was a blankness of sound. I strained to see if I could hear any thing, but I was not able

Faith of a Child

to even hear my own heart beating. I looked around to see if any one else had noticed the change and saw others looking around as well. I looked to my mom, who was dealing with her own emotions and still trembling. As I reached for her, something caught my attention. I saw a shadow, something that I had not seen since I arrived. I heard off in the distance someone scream. As suddenly as it was there, it was gone. What was that? I wondered. I felt a new terror arrive.

Something began to appear before me. It was that mist again. I felt a calling from within the mist. Was it a voice? Or was it more of a thought process of my own?

I once again reached for my mother and while holding her hand; stood, and she and I, like the others around us, turned our attention to the mist and watched in apprehension. I wondered,

"Had she heard the same voice?"

"Was she seeing and feeling the same as I was?"

"What about the others in the area?"

Did they too, see what I was seeing and feel what I was feeling at the same time? Or did each person here seem to be viewing and experiencing their own private hell?

I was sobbing uncontrollably and nothing I felt, could ever bring me comfort again. "Why?" I asked myself.

"Why was I here?"

"Why did I have to see this horrible childhood that I had tried so hard to forget?"

"Why would anyone want me to feel this way?"

"Why would God allow this?"

"What was his plan, his purpose?"

"Didn't he know how hard it was for me to be standing in this place?"

I was not divine. I was living in the flesh! This was too much for me to bear.

Why wouldn't anyone answer me?!

I fell to my knees sobbing. I remembered all of the years that I had spent in counseling, trying to forget that childhood nightmare. "**AND FOR WHAT**" I yelled at no one.

Right now, I had uncontainable feelings of pain and anguish. I felt every scar that a child gets as she grows and learns that everything in life is not fair, and that you just have to learn to deal with it. My parents used to say, "You have the same skin to get glad in", but try as I could, this was something that I just could not get past. I remained on the floor in a puddle of tears and pain.

I heard a male voice spitefully say,

"*Has your God forsaken, left you here to deal with this alone?*"

I screamed at the voice, **"Leave me alone!"**

I tried to stop crying, but the more I tried, the more tears there were. I felt a distant memory trying to emerge and I tried to remember a time when I was still innocent. I could not; no matter how hard I tried, fully grasp that feeling again. I knew I was lost to

Faith of a Child

what ever was about to happen. I didn't care any more. I just did not feel like I could go on.

I sobbed as I wondered, "How am I supposed to have the faith of a child when I don't know what that is any more? Had God really forsaken me and left me to deal with this alone?"

"**Oh God**" I wailed, "HELP ME!"

I do not know where it came from, but I felt a rush of warmth surround me and heard a soft voice in the mist tell me, "Children are the perfect unblemished gift from God". My choking sobs slowed a bit and the voice went on to say, "Children come into this world as a clean slate. They are a chance for you to experience the lesson of unconditional love that was the original plan that God had for his creation. New parents hold this precious gift and look at the baby with a love so deep they wonder where it comes from. It is called bonding, and it is the one time in your life that you truly know and understand what unconditional love is. It is a moment; a breath of time that soon passes and you will soon begin to forget that lesson."

I struggled to my feet, harshly wiping the tears away, and as I stood there, the mist once again shimmered and within the mist, I saw that special time when the connection of child and God is there, as God infuses the parents with love for this gift. Suddenly I was surrounded with a sweet smell. I tried to place it. I breathed it deeply. "What did it remind me of, I wondered?" Then I knew. It was the smell that makes a grown man fall to his knees in tears, and

Susan Lamar Blish

makes a woman spend the rest of her life reliving that one moment again and again. It was *"new baby smell"*. Not that nasty diaper or spit up smell, but that one that with no rational thought, strikes a cord within you on such an emotional level, that it causes you to want to hold, protect, and love the new baby. You want to cry at the force of the feelings. You don't know where the smell is coming from, but its there, with every baby. Innocence. That's what it was. I actually smelled innocence again.

Just as I was breathing in that love and the emotional charge it gave me, the mist moved again and the voice once again said, *"Children are born into sin."* I knew this. I had been taught in Sunday school that we all are. The voice went on to say "Children have no knowledge of this, and thusly are open to God". It is at the age of reckoning that this changes. This begins the separation of man from his creator. This is not God's choice it is yours alone. You walk away from the one thing that can save you. God removed the veil from your eyes. It is from that time on, that if you truly want to remain in the protection of God, you need to seek him, and his love and forgiveness.

I have always believed that God sends children guardian angels that watch over them from the moment they are born until they begin to loose that innocence. Once we begin to loose the simple faith of a child, we forget, and our angels weep because we no longer seek their help.

Faith of a Child

I paced back and forth in my little square. "Where does the ability for children to believe in the unknown come from" I wondered. All children have the uncanny skill to explain the unknown. They don't question reality. Just ask any child to explain to you who Santa Claus is, or who the tooth fairy is, or better yet, have them tell you who Noah was, or why it rains. To them, something as simple as a box can become a ship, or a clubhouse. Ask a small child some day, to take you for a ride into their world of make believe. They have faith that comes from the innocent state of being.

I asked myself, "Is it possible to get that innocence of faith back once its gone?

Is that what I was supposed to do?" My mind reeled with new thoughts.

As I wondered about my childhood and all of the memories I had just re-experienced, and all that was happening and my being here, I noticed a movement out of my left eye. I looked and saw... no...it couldn't be...JUDY! **"That's impossible,"** I thought! She was make-believe! She did not approach me, but smiled at me and simply said, *"The time is fast approaching; soon you will need to have the faith of a child once again."*

Susan Lamar Blish

Chapter 3

"…Because you are

Lukewarm, neither hot nor cold

I am about to spit you out of my mouth"

(NIV Revelation 3:16)

THE TWO MEN

I stood there with a tear-stained face and tried to catch my breath. I wondered if I was loosing my mind. How could a childhood make believe playmate, be real? I stared at Judy for a moment with my mouth open, then I saw the mist shimmer as if it was beckoning me again. I turned to look at it, and two men appeared to come out of the mist and were suddenly a short distance before me. The first one was holding what appeared to be a scepter in his left hand. It was beautiful in its simplicity. I gauged it to be about 2 feet long and had a design at the top of it that looked like a crown of sorts. The man frightened me for no reason other than the way he looked at me. This man had the demeanor of one that had power.

The second figure appeared much like the first. In his right arm, he held a book. It was quite large and appeared to weigh about fifteen pounds and reminded me of one of the large dictionaries that you see at the library. I noticed writing on the cover, but could not understand the strange design, and wondered what it held.

Both men were of similar height that I gauged to be about 6 feet tall and looked to be about the same weight. The first one had hair that was long, black and wavy, the second one had hair that was about shoulder length as well but was straight and blond. I noticed that their hands were worn with what appeared to be many years of work.

Both men, other than a simple sash they were wearing that were of different colors, were dressed alike. The first man had a

Susan Lamar Blish

sash that came from his left shoulder across to his waist on his right side and it was of a brilliant, almost cobalt blue. The second one was just the opposite, with his starting on his right shoulder and coming to his left side and his sash that was of a deep crimson red. There was strange writing on the sashes as well and looked to be the same as the writing on the book the one man held. Otherwise, their clothing was much the same as I had on comprising of a simple white robe. Both men had golden bands across their foreheads. At first look, it appeared that they had no additional adornment and were of a simple design. As I looked at the bands more closely, I then noticed that they each had what appeared to be a symbol or a number on them. I knew that these men were special, but the reason why eluded me.

They did not speak, but when they appeared, a new calmness settled over the room.

I felt their eyes lock onto me and they began to walk side by side in my direction. It appeared that I was their target. I was surprised they had singled me out; I felt no kinship to them. I watched them as they walked toward me and noted that they did not have any expression on their faces. I did not see them blink or look to the left or the right. As they came close to me, I felt flushed. It was as if a heat was rising to my face from an unknown source. I felt a slight lightheadedness as they approached. They radiated a power; I felt it long before they reached me. My pulse quickened.

Faith of a Child

My hands started to sweat and I was bewildered. What was it they wanted from me?

The closer they got to me, the more I felt I knew them. The one that had the scepter in his hand stopped just a few feet in front of me. His eyes narrowed a bit as he stared at me with unblinking eyes. His eyes were as black as coal and I sensed something from him that made me very uncomfortable. It was as if he could see through me and knew me to my core. I did **not** like him being that close to me. The one that had the book was everything the first one was not. His eyes were full of warmth and yet he looked at me with eyes that were full of sorrow. I wondered, "Was that a tear in his eye? What could make him so unhappy?" Locked in my block of light, I marveled at the difference in these two men and waited for them to approach me.

They started to move toward me again and came to a stop on either side of me. I felt something strange, a pulling sensation that started in the region of my heart. I was suddenly lifted off of my feet and was facing the opposite direction. I was being taken away from the room. For reasons that I did not understand or comprehend at that time, I had been selected for something. Where were they taking me, and why had I been chosen?

I felt small in the presence of these two, and felt there was something about them that I would never understand no matter how long I was in their company. Something told me not to fight the

Susan Lamar Blish

feelings I was having and that they would not hurt me. My instinct told me that they were here to teach me something.

As we moved, I felt a new calm and I was not afraid for the first time since my whole ordeal started.

I turned my head to look back at where I had been and I saw the mist move a bit; I saw my mother fall to her knees and cover her face with her hands. I cried out, wanting to comfort her, but we were moving quickly away from the room.

I wondered where we were going and looked forward to see if I could gain any insight, but we were moving at such a speed that every thing was a blur. The two men did not speak to me, and I had yet to form any questions for them. I was shocked at what was happening. Nothing about this whole thing was making any sense and the longer I was here the less sense it made.

I turned my head and looked back again as we moved. The full size of the room came into view and I gasped at the enormity of it. It seemed to go on for thousands of miles in all directions. I was going to ask the two men about it, but when I looked left and right at the two men, I saw that they were still looking forward.

We came to a stop, and I saw the stars and the planets and in the distance, the earth for the first time. The scene was breathtaking. I could actually feel a pulsing. It felt like a heartbeat. I finally understood what scientist mean when they say "the universe is alive" because I felt the actual life and breath of the universe as it moved and I cried out at the feelings and beauty of it all.

Faith of a Child

The man with the scepter looked at me and said in a very deep voice, *"Child of God, do you know where you are?"* I was too startled at the question to speak and simply shook my head no.

"This" he said with a wave of his hand, **"Is where you will find the truth you seek."**

He raised the hand holding the scepter and looked at me then looked out into the heavens. He raised his right arm, clenched his fist, and with a loud voice cried out what sounded like *"NASAG! DABAQ!"*

I cringed and looked at him shocked by the anger within the sound of his voice. I did not understand the words, and I did not like the sound of them.

Before I had the chance to ask any questions, the other man looked at me and said in a firm voice, ***"Child of God, do you know who you are in relation to God and the rest of His creations?"***

I lowered my head and simply said, "I know that He created us".

I saw a tear once again in his eye. As I listened to the man's voice, I caught my breath; I was ashamed to have answered the way that I did.

I looked at the man, and asked him, "Who are you? What are those words?"

The man looked at me and said with such power in his voice that I choked back a sob as he began to speak. He said, "You could not pronounce our names as they have been given to us by The Ancient of Days. We are messengers. It is not time yet for you to

Susan Lamar Blish

stand before The One True and Only Living God, therefore, we have been instructed by He Who Lives Forever to help you in your search.

The words that you hear mean this:

The first one Dabaq means many things, to fight, threaten, or warn.

The second one Nasag means: Overtake."

He is the voice of Lucifer. He is fulfilling his obligation and purpose and is telling the minions of God to prepare. Soon there will be a battle over your souls. I am here to instruct you on the things you have forgotten.

What you are hearing Child of God, is a calling to arms.

Having attended church as a child, I knew about the final battle of Armageddon that was written about in the Bible. It was the war that is to take place at the end of times, and asked if this was what he was referencing.

He looked at me. "No", He said in a very matter of fact voice".

The way he said "no" was so final, I blanched and stood silent for a moment. I started to ask for more information, but he would not explain further. I was not about to ask the first man.

The two men stood silent for a short time looking off into the distant heavens as if they were listening to something. I strained to listen but did not hear anything. They were not talking to me at the moment so I tried to take in everything that I was being shown and told, and tried to focus on any lessons that they were trying to

42

Faith of a Child

impart on to me. My mind was blank and soon drifted. I had a hard time understanding why had I been singled out. What was so special about me?

I was suddenly brought back when the man began to speak again. He told me I was never alone and I was about to be shown many things; that I must remember and understand for my very soul was on the line. As he spoke, I noticed that the same mist that I had seen in the room was here as well. The mist moved and just as I had been in the room, I was compelled to look at it.

For some reason, the scene appeared differently this time. As I stood with these two men in silence, I heard a small whisper. Gradually the whisper became a voice and I listened to a little girl praying to God. *"Dear Jesus, I've been trying to be as good as I can. Mommy said that I'm a little angel and you are always here. I'm sorry if I have been bad"*.

As I listened to the simplicity of her prayer, I was swept up in the sound and sincerity of it and I wept. As I listened, she was asking God about His day, and were the angels being good. She wanted to know if she was really good, when she grew up, could she be a big angel too. As I listened more, I heard other voices praying the innocent prayers of children. I heard the little girl's voice change and soon, I heard my own voice coming from the mist. As I listened, I heard myself ask all of the questions I had poised to God throughout my entire life.

Why did we feel so alone at times?

Susan Lamar Blish

Why had he allowed something to happen?

Had I actually learned anything from what I had seen and been through?

Was my life all that different from most other peoples?

What had been the most profound lesson of my life to that point?

Did God have a plan for us?

Why would he reveal himself to our forefathers but not to us?

Why didn't we see the same type of miracles that were once commonplace?

The mist shimmered and the man again reminded me, that we are not alone, that God created the beginning of life, and the end. He knows everything. Even to the ends of human existence.

While I was listening to the mist recount my dreams and prayers to God, the two men moved back to each side of me. I reached out to the mist trying to hold on to that moment but, slowly, we began our decent back to the room. I felt my heart breaking as we moved. For some reason, I felt safe listening to those prayers from a child. For reasons that I did not understand, I felt a loss so deep and profound that once again, the tears came and would not stop.

Faith of a Child

CHAPTER 4

"…Jesus Wept"

(NIV John 11:35)

Susan Lamar Blish

THE MIST

I wiped the tears from my eyes and attempted to slow them a bit and catch my breath. I was back in the room, to where I had been a short time ago. I looked around to see if anyone had noticed that I had been gone.

Had I actually been gone or was this more of the mist and its imagery?

I hated this feeling of confusion that seemed to come with not understanding.

I sighed and as I once again settled into the feelings of the room, I saw that Judy was still standing not far off to one side of the mist.

"Was she really there," I wondered? I looked at my mother. I wanted her to actually see the make believe friend that I had as a child. Calling out to my mother, I could see that she was still watching the mist and I could not get her attention, and when I turned back, Judy was gone.

"I knew it", I thought to myself. She WAS just make-believe.

I heard that evil laughter again and once again shivered at the sound of it.

I felt drained from the emotional upheaval that I had been going through. "Would it ever stop" I wondered.

The mist moved once again and I turned to see what it had to show me this time. I glanced at my mother who had not spoken to me the whole time she was there.

Faith of a Child

She was still watching the mist, and I wondered at the look on her face. What was she seeing? Did she see her childhood? Did she feel fear, frustration, and apprehension? What ever it was, she was not talking to me about it and I didn't focus on her.

The mist was now ever present but not actively showing me any thing even though others were watching it and I thought about what I had seen. I wondered why I was so confused by some things and so moved by others. "Maybe," I thought, it was seeing Judy again, or the chance given me to relive a portion of my childhood. Maybe it was a chance to remember even if just for a moment, a time when the world was good and I was an innocent child. It had if nothing else been a time when I did not have to focus on the pains of being an adult.

I sighed in frustration and at the sorrow I was feeling. This was really just a bad dream, wasn't it? "Yes", I told myself it had to be. God has a great sense of humor doesn't he? "Yes," I reminded myself, "He created humor." "Good" I reasoned, and then I knew I would be able to wake up eventually and all of this would be great conversation with my friends. Yes, I could just hear them now, "Tell us the part again about..." and then we would all laugh about it. That had to be the plan all along.

I started talking to myself. Arguing with myself was more like it. I told myself, "You have the ability to control your response to your surroundings. No one else has the right or ability to make you feel anything!" That sealed it. I would refuse to participate any more in this bizarre dream. I would just force myself to wake up. If I had to look at things differently from now on, so be it!

With that decision made, I likened my emotional well being to one of hunger pains or, perhaps a craving was more like it. I needed to feed the pain to make it go away. In the past, that always seemed to work for me, feed the pain, so, why not again?

Yes, I told myself, perhaps it had been good that I did have to remember, and relive that pain of being a child. I shrugged and shook my head. I had no idea when the dream would stop, but I felt that I would certainly have a better grasp of my emotional response to things. "This dream" I told myself, would be great conversation but nothing more. I would not allow it! I heard the voice of my counselors in the past saying "Take charge of your response, no one can make you feel anything. It's how YOU choose to respond that matters".

I heard a gasp and turned to look at my mother. She was pointing to the mist, a look of shock on her face. As I turned to look at what she was pointing to, the two men that I had seen earlier arrived and walked from the mist. Once again, they walked up to me. It finally occurred to me that my mother had not seen the men arrive earlier.

I felt the same uneasiness that I had earlier when they arrived and this time, without hesitation, the man with the book stopped directly in front of me. His arms came up and he opened the book he was holding. He read something from the book that I did not

Faith of a Child

understand, and I felt that same pull again. We arrived back at the same place we had been a short time ago.

The mist was still present here as well, and as I looked at the mist, I was surprised at the change I saw. The mist thickened for a moment, almost as if it were a fog of the same intensity that people often describe as "Thick as Pea Soup". Then just as suddenly it seemed to dissipate slightly and looked less solid.

As the mist took on a new form, we were drawn back from it and I saw clearly that the vessel of my vision was a teardrop. The man with the book began to speak and said to me "Child of God, what you see as the mist, is a tear of God". I was stunned. It had ***never*** occurred to me that God would cry. I knew that Jesus had cried, as I had read it in the Bible, but GOD, the creator of everything?! Never!

I had a clear view of the tear drop and saw within the tear, a full choir of angels, singing and shouting. I stood motionless, frozen to my spot with my mouth open, stunned by the beauty and sound. I saw and heard thousands upon thousand of angels singing within that one tear of God. The sight of this vision moved me to the core of my soul and I was shaken from within and felt a warmth I have never known before envelope me. I cried copious tears and found that I had no choice but to fall to my knees never loosing sight of the image before me. With all the beauty and sound surrounding me, I wanted to remain there, within the safety and serenity of this breathtaking vision.

Susan Lamar Blish

I listened to the sweetest sound I had ever heard with a new awakening within my heart. I felt my heart swell and it was as if my heart would burst within me. I listened to the reverberation as it rose and fell with such intensity that I knew without question it was a song of praise and glory to God. Then, I heard something within the song. I strained to single out the new sound and it finally dawned on me. That new sound was children singing and laughing. This brought a new round to tears to my eyes. I laughed and cried at the same time. It was as if I had never before heard children laugh and sing. I was on an emotional high that I prayed would never leave!

I had not noticed that the two men were again standing on each side of me until one of them spoke. The first one, the one with the scepter once again raised his fist into the air. As he took a step forward toward the mist, he looked at the choir of angles; again he yelled those words that I could not pronounce but did understand, ***"DABAQ! NASAG!"***

I looked at the man, knowing what the words meant and heard the hate raising within his voice, and I cowered at the sound of it. I felt the deepest sense of foreboding.

As he spoke, the mist moved and the choir of angels was gone from my view. With the choir now out of site, I reached out and a small whimper escaped. I did not want to loose that vision or sound. The sudden separation was speaking volumes to me at that

Faith of a Child

moment. I felt a deepening sense of loss. I looked at the one man and then the other.

I stared at the men not understanding, and suddenly the man with the book began to speak as if he knew what I was going to ask. He told me that God was not unlike us and He feels our pain and understands our sorrow. I looked toward the mist again and I began to see within that one drop, all of the pain that God has suffered because of the choices of man through all of time.

I saw within the tear, the beginning of time, when God, from nothing but his thought, started life. I saw God create man and his reasons for it, I saw the fall of man in Eden, and the tear in Gods eye that came from that fall. Within this tear I saw how we had walked away from God at every point in our life, and only as children did we run with a smile on our faces and look for and see God in everything. I wept as I saw the tears of God sweep over the earth as he cried for a world of sinners that was now lost. I saw the renewal of the earth and then with innocence, how a cloud was alive to a child and how the angles were sent by God at every point in our life to assist us. OH! how they rejoiced when we returned. Then, within the tear, once again I saw war, famine, plagues, the homeless and the hungry. I saw how we have walked away from our brother at every turn. I saw as well, how we have rejected God and His plan for us. I was shocked when I saw how the angels cried at the death of a child that could have been prevented by the intervention of any of us. I saw how little we cared. I fell to my

Susan Lamar Blish

knees sobbing at the pain and guilt I felt. Then, I was shown the ending. I stared through my tears at the mist and saw the end of war, the end of pain, the end of all of the hate that we have so carefully cultivated over all of the years, and finally the end of the separation of God and his children.

I felt naked and exposed before my creator, and I did not like being in this spot. I fidgeted a bit as the man was talking. I had to admit to myself, that this insight was something I had never given thought to before. I wondered if I had really ever given any thought to what God wanted. Was I so selfish and self serving that I was not able to see or hear God's desire for me?

The man continued to talk and said with a voice so full of love that I began to cry harder at the sound of it, "God created you for Himself. You are His child. The mist that you see here and within the realm of the room, are Gods tears. Within the mist, you have seen what God sees. He cries as you do. He loves as you do. He has sent His son to teach you love, to bring you home, because He has forgiven you. You were created in innocence but lost the faith needed to return to God. This is the time that you need to once again, call on that faith and be his child."

My tears would not stop as he was speaking. It was as if with his voice alone, he could call me to redemption. For some reason, my heart felt heavy. My emotions took on a new feeling and I allowed that feeling to stir within me. As I felt that stirring within my heart, I felt warmth surround me. I wondered, "Can I have that

Faith of a Child

childlike faith again?" Is it possible to actually believe as a child again, or have I become so hardened that no matter what I do, I will never feel that again?"

With that thought, I was back in the room, standing next to my mother.

Susan Lamar Blish

CHAPTER 5

"My heart says of you,

Seek his face!

Your face Lord, I will seek"

(NIV Psalm 27:8)

THE VEIL

I stood for a moment in bewildered silence. The tears had once again, at least for the moment, slowed. "Would they ever stop," I wondered?

I sighed, not out of frustration, but because I felt different somehow. There was a new feeling within my heart. This felt different from the awakenings or stirrings that I had felt in the past. I didn't know what was different about the feeling this time but I hoped it was real. "Will this hold out" I wondered. Are these feelings true or is it just another passing renewal?" I cried again at the desperation I was feeling, and prayed that this was the real thing. "Would God allow me to keep wondering or would I hear an answer to my prayer this time? Had I just not been listening in the past?"

I reflected on the relationship I'd had with God. I never had a problem asking God for forgiveness, but that end part, the acceptance had always been the problem. I believed in God, and in Jesus. That was not a problem. Why did I think that this would be any different? Did I really WANT it to be different; did I believe it COULD be different?

I felt like a war was raging inside of me. On one side was that voice that yelled, your friends will laugh at you if you do this. If you accept this story you will become a fanatic and none of your friends will ever talk with you again! Is that what you want? You've tried this before and you know that it's not real. If it was, why didn't you believe it then? Why did you walk away? The other side was just as

Susan Lamar Blish

strong. It was telling me, in the past, I had not fully embraced or accepted the gift of forgiveness. And yes, it was a gift. I was a baby in my walk with God. No one asked me if I had any questions, and when I did try and ask questions, I was told that I didn't need to know the answer then, I'd find out when I was in heaven. So as a result, I felt that if I did all of the right things, I was saved. And I did try to do the right things, by volunteering my time and energies, thinking that as long as people said that I was saved, then I was. But something had always been lacking, a chance for my faith, to grow. I never gave God a chance. I never looked beyond that first step. I honestly didn't know there was more.

I was glad that the two men were still there because I had so many questions I wanted to ask them.

The room had new warmth in it, which seemed to radiate from an unknown source. It was as if the warmth was in everything, WAS everything. I wondered to myself if the two men were the cause of the warmth, though I did not feel compelled to ask them

A hush fell over the room and everyone in it was suddenly stilled. I looked around trying to see if I could locate the reason for the quietness. "Now what was happening?" I wondered.

I noticed that within the mist a new vision had started. I frantically searched for the angels within it but they were not there this time. As I stared into the vision before me I was told by the one man that had previously done all of the talking, "Child of God, it is time for you to see and understand the truth."

Faith of a Child

I looked at him quizzically and searched his face and his eyes as he spoke. "God has opened your eyes. You are being allowed to see the veil that was placed before you at birth." "Veil?" I wondered, "What are you talking about?" I asked him; "What veil?" He looked directly at me almost **through** me as he continued to speak ignoring my questions, "You were innocent. The Ancient of Days allowed the removal of the veil when you reached the age of understanding. It is now your choice to seek Him and His will in your life."

I wanted to tug on his robe at that moment and yell, "Excuse me!" But instead I formulated my questions a bit calmer though I am not sure where this calm came from. "What veil? What are you talking about?

Why would God do such a thing?

Why would He place a veil over our eyes and hide Himself from us?"

I asked these questions in rapid succession, looking for an answer.

For some reason I felt that deep guilt from my childhood again and I demanded, "Is that why He never answered me when I called on Him?" I desperately wanted shift this guilt to someone else, and if God had hid himself from me, well then, He was going to get the burden of guilt that I had carried for years.

At times I felt as if this man was able to see right through me, knew what I was thinking and feeling and knew what I was going to

57

Susan Lamar Blish

ask even before I formulated the questions in my mind. He shifted a bit with his huge book and continued speaking to me.

He told me that it is not that God hides himself from us, but that we are protected within the folds of His robe until we reach an age of understanding. He seemed to slowly move to his right so that I could see past him while he spoke. I began to see what appeared to be mountains and valleys behind him in the mist. He went on to explain that just as a new mother would protect her child from the cold by wrapping her baby in a blanket, so our Father, The Ancient of Days keeps us safely within the folds of His robe. As I looked on he continued speaking, "You are close to His heart and protected there."

He again moved slightly and I noticed that the scene behind him changed and appeared to pull back in a way that I was able to view more of the vision. I began to clearly see that what I had perceived as mountains and valleys were in fact the folds of an iridescent colored and ever moving robe! I looked on in amazement and within the robe, I saw children running, laughing and playing. They appeared to be hugging and clinging to the robe. I looked up at the man before me, not understanding and he directed my attention back to the scene behind him.

As I looked into the mist, I saw the hands of God. I thought to myself almost at the same time I was seeing it... "The hands of God" almost whispering in my mind over and over again... "The hands of God." I fell prostrate and still before the vision, before my

Faith of a Child

Creator. Then once again I began to hear the choir of angels singing and shouting. Oh, how, my heart skipped a beat at that sound. I wanted to leap to my feet and get just one more glimpse of that heavenly choir. I wanted to shout out with joy and join them in singing praises to God, but all I could do was lay there and weep for the loss that was so profound in my heart. I felt it would totally consume me. I felt that I was not worthy of this, and that I would never be able to join them in their singing.

As I lay there with this scene before me, I felt a new stillness within my soul. I reached out with a tentative hand desperately wanting to touch the robe of God, my Father one again. However, before I could touch the robe, slowly, the vision dissipated and the man with the book once again called me to my feet. I wanted to just lie there and weep, but instead I managed to get myself shakily to my feet.

He began to explain to me that we are a protected virtue behind this veil, the robe of the Almighty God and that it defines the truth for us and allows us the freedom to be God's children. When we are safely within the robe, we are innocent. However, a time comes that the king of this earth takes over and the veil is removed, sometimes by force. We are pulled away from God and must begin our journey of seeking Him. God allows the way the veil is removed because it is required.

I looked at the man and asked him, "When is the veil removed?" He did not answer my question but continued with his narrative. I

Susan Lamar Blish

saw in the mist, the journey of the masses to the temple and the Kings of the Ancient Empires talking to the priests of the temple. My guide was telling me, "In the beginning of the day' of man, priests were given the job of making amends for you. It was their job to make the sacrifices and acted as a go between when it came to matters of the soul and your being allowed to come before God. But, when the Son of God came to walk among you, He was given the task of being the only sacrifice that God would accept from that point on.

The man with the scepter who had been silent all this time suddenly spoke, "Child of God, you are beginning to understand that you need to make a choice. This is something that you must do alone and of your free will. But, know this; your lack of choice **_IS_** a choice. You must freely choose to serve God or you **_WILL_** serve the king of your earth and his desires for all eternity."

I still did not fully understand the concept of this veil and why God would remove a veil of protection and leave us exposed. Something seemed to be missing.

The man with the book looked at me as if reading my mind and said, "The age the veil is removed happens long before the age of reckoning. It is not God's will that you loose your innocence, it is the will of man that takes it from you."

I glanced over at the mist for a moment and I saw children playing. "Were they the key?" I wondered? I started to ask the man, but asked instead, "How does God remove this veil?" He looked

Faith of a Child

down at me and with his eyes filled with tears, his voice cracking, he said in almost a whisper, "With His tears child, with His tears."

I looked up at this huge powerful looking man with his large book, frightened by the tears in his eyes. Overcome with confusion and a feeling in my heart of wrenching sadness that I am not able even at this time to find words to describe, I asked him if he could explain what he meant. He pointed toward the mist, "It is not that God removes you from His robe; it is man that forces this removal." As I watched, I saw within the mist something I had not seen before. I saw before me a great tear fall and join many others in a river, I saw the great robe of God and I heard a mighty voice cry out, "Another one has been taken from us!"

I turned to the man with a pain in my heart and just stared up at him. He explained that these tears are the river of life and one day those that accept will return and will all drink from it again. That these tears are the waters that feed the Tree Of Life and just as God allowed Adam and Eve the choice to eat of the tree and open their eyes so it is also required for us to seek God and His will in our lives now.

I wept at the loss and understanding I was beginning to feel.

This was a new beginning for me.

As I looked around the room I sensed a new kinship with some of the people here with me, yet, it seemed something was still missing… a coming together. I was unsure how I knew this or how this was supposed to happen, but felt that I would soon find out.

Susan Lamar Blish

Chapter 6

"Restore to me the joy of your salvation

And grant me a willing spirit, to sustain me"

(Psalm 51:12)

Faith of a Child

Redemption

Part I

As I reflected on what the man had told me, I noticed that many of the people in the area closest to me had a different look about them, one that seemed like serenity or a look of wonderment. I looked at them with joy in my heart and wondered, had they seen and felt what I was seeing and feeling? Many others, however, still had that same look, that showed fear and confusion.

As I was looking around, the mist moved and again I was drawn to look at it. The man looked at me and said, "All you need to do Child of God is call on Him. He will forgive you." I looked at the man and said, "I don't know if I can ever have that simple faith again."

I had always been taught that once you are past childhood, you must put away childish things. Isn't that what the Bible tells us?

He pointed my attention back to the mist and I saw within the mist, all of the times that I had called on God to save me, and all of the times that I had walked away from Him. "Why, I asked the man, "Why do I always manage to leave things to God to handle, only to take them back as if he could not handle them?" As I looked at a portion of my past once again, I felt that God would never be able to forgive me for those things and that I was truly lost.

The vision was shattered when I heard a wail of such pain and anguish that it seemed to reverberate across the whole of the room.

Susan Lamar Blish

The man looked at me and then I realized that *I* was making this sound. As the tears came in rivers, I fell to my knees and covered my face with my hands. I cried out, "What's keeping me from giving myself to God again…what could keep me from the one thing that I knew could bring me peace?"

The man called to me and said, "Look." He pointed to the mist. I saw through my tears within the mist what appeared to be an altar. It had four golden legs sitting on top of ball feet of the same gold. It held the base of the altar about two feet off of the ground. On the sides were inlaid in a highly polished deep colored wood that I thought to be gems of various colors which created an intricate design or writing. It was beautiful. On top it held a golden crown that sat atop of a small pillow. Along side of the crown were a scepter and a small scroll that had writing on it. I did not understand the writing, but it looked to be the same as I had seen on the man's book.

As if he could read my mind, my guide nodded his head and said, "Yes, What you see on the altar are the vestments of our Risen Lord, the Crown of our Lord Jesus, the Scepter that He holds in his hand to rule the nations and the Scroll that only He is worthy to open to judge all people.

Then once again as I looked at the mist, I saw what looked to be a vast expansion of mountains and valleys. I heard the sound of children laughing and looked to the man and said, "I don't understand". The man pointed back to the mist and the mist blurred

Faith of a Child

a bit then as it cleared, I saw within the mist, a sun rising from behind a hill. As I looked, I saw a series of three crosses standing on the hill. As I looked at the scene before me, I saw a small pool of red that looked like blood at the base. I turned to look at the man asking with my look, if this was what I thought it to be. He did not answer me but simply looked at me.

I reached out and touched the blood. My heart felt as if it was breaking and I cried out "GOD, PLEASE FORGIVE ME!" As my fingers touched that small pool of blood, I heard a new voice crying out saying, "**Glory to God**" and I heard another voice shouting, "**One of our flock has returned!**"

I stayed there kneeling at the feet of God. I felt such a renewal within my soul. I accepted that I was finally forgiven. I knew then that nothing would ever again shake my faith in God.

I was finally, once again, safely within the robe of God.

My tears fell in rivers at the renewed freedom. I did not know if I could contain the feelings that I now felt with in my heart. All I wanted to do was to stay there kneeling at the feet of my Creator and sing praises to Him and never stop. I knew that nothing would ever come between this feeling of freedom again.

Slowly the mist faded away and the man looked at me. I stood up trembling with the new emotion and tears streaming down my face. He smiled at me for the first time and said, "Believe as the child he created, and know that it is real."

Susan Lamar Blish

I looked at the man slightly puzzled by his words, and as I started to give the man a hug of thanks, without warning, the second man, the one with the scepter, looked at me his eyes narrowing. He shouted at me, "**PREPARE YOUR SELF CHILD OF GOD".** I started to recoil at the sound of his voice when I froze in my spot with a renewed terror that rumbled throughout my body. I felt *doubt.*

I stared at both men with my mouth open not knowing what to say when they moved forward toward me once again; I was suddenly back in the room. They had disappeared.

Faith of a Child

Chapter 7

"You believe there is one God. Good!

Even the demon's believe that— and shudder."

(NIV James 2:19)

Susan Lamar Blish

THE DEMONS

Within my heart I still felt that new warmth and these tears that stained my face would not leave. I felt that I had finally been saved. I wanted to share with my mom what I had just experienced but she had a look of amazement on her face and I just could not bring myself to interrupt her thoughts.

I looked for the mist but it had dissolved and was gone and there was no sign of it anywhere. I turned around to see if the men had reappeared and ask if they could tell me what had happened but they were gone.

I felt alone and abandoned and screamed out "NO!!!" I needed them there to help me. They couldn't just leave me, not like this!!! I knew that I could not do this alone.

I stood along with the multitude in a confused restlessness. I did that mental checklist of hands, arms, feet, what was working, what was missing, trying to take in what had just happened, and for a brief moment, everything felt calm. My heartbeat slowed a bit and I knew I had to get a grip on my emotions.

I looked at the others in the room, wondering if they too were as shocked by what had just taken place as I was.

Suddenly, I saw with alarm, all of the children, in stark contrast to the obvious horror of the adults around me, smile. The children ran and played with lack of restraint. They seemed to be unaffected by all of this. They ran back and forth across the room singing a song that I could not understand, to a spot in what I thought looked

68

Faith of a Child

to be the middle of the room. A few of the adults were also singing this song and they too went to that same place in the room. The place was brighter than the rest of the area and a radiant light that was almost blinding, engulfed them. I watched them smile and laugh with delight. They seemed to be talking with someone or something and the sweet sound of their child laughter was music to my ears and lifted my frightened and tired soul. I wanted so desperately to join them, yet was not able to move from the spot that I had arrived back in.

As I tried to drink in the sound of the children laughing and playing, there was a dampening of sound. I could not hear anything at that moment, yet desperately wanted to know how they could be happy and smiling…. Suddenly I heard that soft voice again say to me;

*"**You must keep the faith of a child.**"*

I still did not understand. What did it mean, "Keep the faith of a child?"

Before I could give it a fleeting thought, something caught my attention. A movement? A shadow? Did I really see any thing?

"NoOo…**wait**…**YES**…!

Breathing…!

I could hear breathing!

I strained to listen and could almost hear what suddenly sounded like the din of conversation across the crowded room. You

Susan Lamar Blish

know people are whispering; yet, this was different, this grew in volume and became thousands of times louder.

Then, just as suddenly, nothing, as suddenly as it had started, it stopped. No sound, *anywhere.* I looked around the room, twisting my body left and right as I tried to see if any one else noticed.

The absence of sound was so loud; it could only be described as the vacuum created by a tornado just before it hits... a cone of silence. You knew that if you screamed, no one could hear you. My heart began to race anew and as I felt it pounding; I thought it was going to burst inside of me.

As the new stillness took hold, a deep feeling of dread fell over the area like a heavy blanket... all those in the room, except the children and those few adults, seemed to feel this. I stood there looking around trying to deny the feeling of alarm, when the sensation of panic totally consumed me.

Something was there*...*

Something touched me!

I froze in my spot, waiting for who knows what. I reached for my mom, who turned to look at me. As we held on to each other for support, a feeling of dread crashed over us. I love my mother with all that I am, and knew that she would be the one that I would naturally call out to in times of pain and troubles as a child. I called to her now with a renewed sense of panic. **"MOM!"** I could not hear myself screaming. I saw her mouth move but did not hear anything coming out

Faith of a Child

What ever this was I didn't want to be there and I wanted my mom to fix it and make it go away! As I looked at my mother and she too was trying to pray and call out. I knew she was as afraid as I was. I could see it in her face as my mind cried out, "**I don't understand any of this!**"

I heard a voice that sent shivers down my spine and I felt a cold hand wrap around my heart as it whispered in my ear:

"I DARE YOU TO MOVE"!

I screamed in my panic and flailed my arms in an attempt to push away or shake off what ever it was that held my heart. My mind yelled, "**RUN!**" but I could not move. I was locked to the spot of light and nothing I did, could budge me.

Through my panic, again I heard that soft voice,

"Have the faith of a child."

I heard some of the others around me screaming and the sound became deafening. Panic had a full grip on me. I screamed, "**OH LORD, PLEASE...HELP!!**"

My heart was beating so fast the sound was pounding in my ears. It sounded like a thunderous waterfall as it fell to the pool of rocks beneath it, and I couldn't control my fear.

As that icy grip held my heart my tears fell fast and hard as I wept.

Suddenly, with no warning, there was a sound so frightening that I fell to the floor, and covered my head with my arms, trying in vain to hide. The sound started off as a very low, deep echoing wail

71

Susan Lamar Blish

of anguish, then, as it increased in volume, it changed and sounded like the cry of a pig being slaughtered combined with the sound of the winter winds on iced over reeds. There was a shriek of pain, and then... a suddenness of vacant air and no sound came forth. The absence of sound was more deafening than that of a thousand airplanes in take off.

I could not control the sobbing as it racked my body. Through eyes that were puffy from tears, I began to notice around me, figures appearing within the confines of the room.

Something told me they were not human. Their quantity was almost unfathomable in number. They were indescribable in appearance, with a beauty that I've yet to see in nature. I prayed that they were angels sent to protect us. .

Over the years, I remember telling people, *"Don't trust that person, there is just something about them I don't like."* It wasn't what they were wearing, or the way they talked, it was more what they *didn't* say that gave them away. The feeling I got from seeing and feeling the presence of these creatures was the same in nature to that feeling.

I got to my feet and with the others in the room stood and looked at the new arrivals as they increased in numbers. We looked at them at length, with awe.

They were indescribable in appearance, with a height that appeared to be over eight feet tall. They had delicately chiseled features. There faces looked almost like a fine porcelain and

Faith of a Child

reminded me of the beautiful statues that the masters had carved hundreds of years ago that now stood in formal gardens and museums. Their eyes were clear and bright and looked to me like the colorful twinkling lights seen at Christmas Time. Their wings towered over them and followed them by a few feet coming to an almond shape at the tips and were light and full with an iridescent color that seemed to change as they moved. Their hair was long and glistening like the morning dew before the sun dried it, reflecting all of the colors of the rainbow and appeared to flow like a light breeze on the water. They had long tapered fingers that one would picture a concert pianist to have. Their clothing was of the same type of robes that we had on and was whiter than snow. The light of the room seemed to reflect off of them, creating a glow in the region of them. I wanted to embrace them and rejoice that they were there.

Then, something about them changed, and a renewed sense of foreboding swept over me. The realization hit me with full force.

" These were not angels to protect us!"

I do not remember their appearance changing as it happened slowly. Almost like the change from day, to twilight. Without my grasping it, they had changed into something that reflected their true nature, something so horrible that the very sight of them made me gasp for air and freeze in my spot with such a fear and horror that I attempted to rebuke them.

Susan Lamar Blish

In what seemed like the blink of an eye, these beautiful creatures seemed to grow in height and towered over us and became horrendous raging monsters. Their clothing was now torn and ragged, and had stains on them and smelled of feces and rotten eggs of such putrid intensity that the smell permeated the air and I wanted to vomit. The long fingers now had the appearance of claws with razor sharp jagged and torn nails. The fingers were deeply cut and black, with open sores that were dripping pus and blood. On their arms, hands and faces, there appeared gashes that were scarlet red and they were covered with scabs that oozed green colored pus that ran down the area in streaks and they showed little sign of healing. Their faces that had held such a radiant smile now held a look that was deeply etched with such anger and hate, that the brows appeared to come to a point above their eyes changing and twisting with each movement they made.

Their eyes were unblinking and were black as coal. I could sense that they had no soul and they held no warmth. I could see that their teeth were long and sharply pointed, and when they spoke or opened their mouths, saliva and vomit dripped from their mouths.

The beautiful wings that I had seen now looked like those you see when a bird has fallen out of its nest. They were twisted, bloody, and missing feathers.

When they moved, I saw what looked like a shadow attached to the creatures and it followed their movements. I thought for a

Faith of a Child

moment that I was seeing things again because it looked to be part of the creature, and then when without warning, the shadow, almost separated from the creatures and turned and looked at me. I saw what appeared to be people and faces within that shadow and knew instantly they were the reflection of lost souls. Cold chills ran down my spine and I tried to look away, but my eyes were firmly fixed on these creatures.

"**Dear God!**" I screamed. I now knew that I was in the presence of..."**DEMONS.**"

I could not lie to myself.

This place was **HELL!**

I heard what could only be described as a powerful gnashing of teeth, the fervor of anger not unlike the sound that a starved lion would make in a wild frenzy of its first kill. It was a crunching and tearing sound that reverberated from every area of the room.

As the sound grew in pitch along with it I heard a thunderous maniacal laughter of glee, in a way that I've never heard before. I pray I never hear it again. It sent a renewed terror into the depths of my soul. The volume made was so enormous that I froze in my spot and placed my hands over my ears to lesson the shock of it, praying it would stop. I wanted to run and hide in fear, but could not move. I felt as if the sun had gone down on a warm afternoon, and the slow darkness began to appear. Before we had the chance to realize it, evil had arrived and we were not protected.

Susan Lamar Blish

A new round of tears started and this time, my whole body shook with the fear and tears that I was shedding.

I kept screaming, "I don't understand!

Why had we been taken to this awful place?

What had I done to make God bring me to this?

Was there no hope for me?"

Then I heard a new voice say in a deep thunderous rumble:

"CHALLENGE THEM."

Faith of a Child

CHAPTER 8

When pride comes,

Then comes disgrace,

But with humility, comes wisdom.

(Proverbs 11:2)

Susan Lamar Blish

Redemption

Part II

The words echoed in my mind. Challenge them.... Challenge them to what?! Who was going to challenge us and what was it we were going to have to do? I stood frozen to my spot and felt the panic once again sweep over me. Would this nightmare never end?!

As I stood there terrified, my heart beating at full speed, the two men that had been with me before, appeared again. As with their arrival before, the people in the room seemed to settle a bit and my tears slowed. I didn't care any more who these men were, I was just glad they had showed up. The sound that the demons made slowly echoed down to one final shriek and the room grew strangely quiet. Looking around the room I saw that the demons were gone and every one stood as they had before the demons had arrived. "I knew it." I thought to myself, "I am loosing my mind".

Once again, with out hesitation, the man with the book took what I now thought of as his place and stood on my left and the man with the scepter stood on my right. It was interesting the comfort that I gained from being close to these two men. For some reason, I always felt calm when they were near me, even though I still had a small amount of apprehension each time I first saw them arrive. Yet, no matter the comfort I gained from the one man, the other man still made me very uneasy.

Faith of a Child

The one that had done most of the talking again opened his book.

I stood on my toes and I tried to look this time to see what it said, but all I saw were little dots covering the pages. He looked to be reading something then looked at me and said "Child of God, our Father, the Ancient of Days has heard your plea."

I looked at the man my heart swelling within me and with new tears in my eyes. I tried to smile a bit hoping he would understand what I was feeling and help me understand these emotions I was having.

I thought about the time that I had been here and wondered if I was ever going to get the chance to put into practice what I had learned. I wondered, had I really learned anything at all?

Before I had the chance to focus on the issues, the mist moved and drew my attention to it.

The man pointed to the mist and began a new narrative. He told me that what I was about to witness was to help me understand that I was still holding on to past things and that because of this, I was not allowing the Glory of God to become a part of me or work in my life. I was not sure that I fully understood what he was talking about. Hadn't I lain at the feet of God and given myself to him? What more was there?

I stood in anticipation and looked to see what the mist would show me this time.

Susan Lamar Blish

The mist took on the form as it had in the past and I began to see myself as a young girl of thirteen. I heard myself thinking as I road my bike, "Well, if they don't love me then I will just see if I can find a new family to live with." I was at a K-Mart store that was just opening. As I watched myself I was drawn back to the day that I had gone to the store. I knew what I would do once I was there, and after locking my bike, I walked into the store and looked around. It wasn't long before I found myself in the stationary department and for no reason other than to see if I could be caught, I took a small box of stationary and placed it in my pocket. It was just a small box of cards, but I wanted them, and I knew if I had asked my parents for money I would get the lecture on how little we had and that this was not something that we could afford at that time.

I felt a wave of guilt pass over me as I watched myself walk out of the store, get back on my bike and ride home. I placed that box, in my room and went about my tasks. At school the next day, I told some of my friends what I had done and laughed about it. I was proud of the fact that I had taken them. I told that story many times to friends over the years, always laughing about what I had done and never once did I feel shame or guilt. The thought of why I had taken them was lost along the years, but watching myself there as a young girl again, brought about a new wave of guilt.

The scene changed and I saw myself a bit older, and I was working in a topless night club. I had a customer that had turned me down when I had asked him if he wanted a dance and the

Faith of a Child

money that night was slow in coming. After about an hour, I noted at his feet, a wedding ring and a neatly folded bundle of money. It was obvious that he had taken off his ring and placed it in his pocket, but it had fallen out along with the money and he had not noticed. I was still angry that he had turned me down and that he had been rude to me while doing it. I walked over to the table and placed my foot over the money hiding it from view, and sat down in a chair that was next to him, and slid the money toward myself and soon had it close to where I could bend over and get it with out making any type of sudden movements that would bring his attention to what I was doing. As one of the other dancers came over, I bent down to adjust my foot into my shoe and picked up the ring and the money and walked away. I walked over to the DJ booth where my boyfriend was working and counted the money. There was over $300.00 there and a wedding ring to boot! SCORE! I knew that I could pawn the ring for a few bucks so the night had not been a total waste of time. I had made my goal for the night and had taken my revenge on the man all at the same time! Just how was he going to explain to his wife that he had no wedding ring and had no pay check? Honestly, I didn't care. I justified my actions by telling myself, "He should have thought of that before he came into the club, right?"

The man had gone to the manager of the club and asked if we could all be checked to see if any of us had the money or ring. This

Susan Lamar Blish

was a common occurrence when men came in and spent more than they had planned to spend and they wanted their money back.

I did ask the manager and the other girls if we found any money if it was a finders keepers thing, and every one agreed that yes, those were the rules. When they asked me if I had the money, I said no, that I did not have it.

He had turned me down and that was the end of it.

It was very common in our small club to make over $300.00 a night, with some nights into the $500.00 or more range. We had always considered it a bad night if we only went home with $100.00!

After the club had closed and we had all gone to our favorite breakfast spot, I told the others what I had done and they all laughed with me. The other dancers told me they would have done the same and were only jealous that they had not been the one to find it.

Looking back, I should have given the money back to the man along with his ring. But standing there, looking at the scene before me, I still felt justified by the actions that I had taken.

I felt a flood of emotion and pain as I watched that time in my life. It had been hard. I was a single mom, raising two kids with no child support from my x-husband and felt that dancing was the easy road to money. I really didn't have a lot of training in any field that would provide for my kids and myself the way that dancing had. My favorite line had become, "Where else can a woman with no

Faith of a Child

training make over $60,000.00 of untraceable cash every year and stay in great shape to?"

Over time, I got to be really good at dancing, and the more I learned, the more money I made. Working in an adult night club and taking off my clothing, changed me. The seedy and dark side of life was very attractive but it changed who I was at the time, changed my views, my values, my morals, and my attitude.

The mist continued to show me all of the times in my life that I had broken the law, had taken things that were not mine, had lied to friends and people that I claimed to love and how I had bragged and made up stories to make myself look better. It showed me the deepest secrets that I had and the darkest moments in my life. I had forgotten so many of the things that I had done that as I saw them again, a new pain was building within me.

The mist continued to show me my past and just how much I had talked about some of those things with my friends over the years and how never once, had I accepted what I had done as wrong. I heard myself laughing about them, laughing at the way I used to get drunk, lie outright to cover for friends or family, not told the whole truth so that I would not have to take responsibility for my actions. There it was in front of me and these two men. The pride I had in doing these things!

I looked at the man with tears in my eyes. I said "I thought that I was forgiven and that all of this was forgotten! Why show me all of this?"

Susan Lamar Blish

The man looked at me and said, "Precious child of God, it is the past that YOU hold on to that causes your confusion and doubt."

I know that the look on my face must have been one of stunned puzzlement, because he continued with his narrative, and I did not try to interrupt but stood still and listened and watched intently. I wanted to know more!

I felt a slight breeze that seemed to almost push part of the mist to one side creating within the vision a new vision. I saw within this new vision a woman on her knees, her hands covering her face weeping and asking God to forgive her and make her clean and new.

As I watched, I felt a tug within my heart as I realized that the woman was myself of just a short time ago. My eyes filled once again with tears as I thought of that moment that seemed to be so long ago. The man shuffled his stance slightly and within the scene before me, I saw a smaller image taking form.

The man looked at me and quietly said "Child it is the past that YOU hold onto that causes your confusion and pain. Immediately as he finished, I realized that my own self-condemnation, my own boastful pride, my own lies and deception to myself and others was hindering my acceptance of God's forgiveness. It was this pride in my past that was keeping me from God. I realized that I did not need to keep asking God for forgiveness for my past. I had asked for forgiveness, and he had granted me that. God had wiped my

Faith of a Child

slate clean. He had taken my sin, just as I had asked him to. It was me... I was holding on to my past, and not letting it go.

The man pointed back to the mist.

I saw just above myself kneeling there a list of every thing that I had confessed to God. The list seemed to go on and on. Every second of my life was recounted before my eyes. Everything that I had done was there, every breath I had taken, every beat of my heart was listed.

Almost as soon as I recognized myself, with a renewed hope, I prayed to God along with the image before me and asked Him to take all of this away. I saw a hand slowly erase the scene before me. The past was gone.

There before me now, was a vision of myself, with the knowledge of my past, and the lessons that I had learned, but the pain was gone. I knew then, that I had asked for and finally accepted my forgiveness and had fully allowed God to make me clean and new. Never again would I carry the burden of that past or that pain. Never again would I brag about the things that I had done to others. Never again would I allow my ego to stand before God and not allow Him the proper place in my heart or my life. He had forgiven me, I had accepted that forgiveness and I had finally, finally been set free.

Susan Lamar Blish

Chapter 9

I baptize you with water,

But he will baptize you with the Holy Spirit."

(NIV Mark 1:8)

Redemption

Part III

I was elated at the freedom within my soul, and my heart sang at the renewal I felt. I knew that I had walked through a dark humid storm that had suppressed my soul and kept me from God. I felt the changing within me. With each passing moment, I was gaining a new understanding, a new insight.

I asked myself "Would I finally be able to put into practice every day of my life all that I had been shown?" I was beginning to understand the plan of salvation that I had heard my whole life and hoped that soon I would be shown the full plan that God had for me.

I did not want this feeling to end! I did not want to go back to who I had been before this. I asked myself "Was I capable of allowing God to fully run my life? Would I stumble and fall as I had in the past?" I pushed the dark thoughts from my mind and relaxed once again.

As I was basking in the feelings that I was experiencing, the mist moved once again and the man pointed with out speaking.

A new scene lay before me and with my head slightly clocked to one side, I watched with renewed interest. Hadn't I asked for and finally accepted my forgiveness? What more was there?

As I looked within the mist, I saw at the end of a very long walk way, a building. It was slightly more than a square, but not what I

Susan Lamar Blish

would call a large rectangle as the sides were just slightly longer than the front. It had four very large white columns evenly spaced in the front starting at the base of the building going all the way to the roof, appearing to hold the roof in place. The building was white and looked to me like it was made of a grant, or sandstone, as it sparkled slightly in the sun. The roof was red in color, and looked to be made of ceramic or clay and the shape of the shingles, being half circle, reminded me of those that I had seen pictured on a lot of the homes in the Mediterranean area and were over lapping. The roof came to a peak at the center, gently sloping from the center peak and had no other color or shape.

At the entrance to the building, was a curtain. It too was a deep red in color, and had a split down the middle.

There were steps at the end of the long walkway, leading up to the entrance of the building that were made of the same white stone that the rest of the building was made of. The building was not one of a showy style, it was actually basic in design but I felt the power it held even from the distance that I judged to be about five hundred feet or so.

As I stood there, the man with the book that had done the majority of the talking read something from his book and said in a commanding voice, "Child of God, you alone are to go into the temple".

I was no longer surprised by his words, and they made perfect sense to me at the time. However, it was still with a slight

Faith of a Child

trepidation, that I walked the long walk to the temple, and climbed the stairs and placed my hand on the curtain. Before I pulled it aside, I turned around to look for conformation that I was doing what I was supposed to, but the men were once again gone.

As I entered the temple, I saw the room was slightly different from the outside. The air was cool and had a slight sweet smell to it, but the room was not cold. I turned around in circles looking at everything and I tried to remember all that I was seeing. The floor was a simple stone ruff cut and gray in color with no pattern to it and I noted that the room was square with large columns as well. The room was two stories inside although I did not see any way to get to the top floor. The columns were about 4 feet around and evenly spaced about six feet apart. They were a dark, highly polished wood with intricate designs of vines and flowers carved into them. On the top floor, between each column, there was a wooden barrier of sorts that was carved into an open fret work design depicting scenes of flowers and birds. As I looked at the columns closer, I noted that there were what appeared to be gilded angels that were about two feet tall with their wings wrapping around the top of the columns. The ceiling was a deep red and had carved gilded arches that met in the center of the room connecting a huge tree that seemed to be the center of the arches. The tree also had flowers and birds on the branches. The whole of the room, the woodwork, columns and barriers all appeared to be part of this tree. I also saw paintings that reminded me of those done in the

Susan Lamar Blish

Sistine Chapel showing what I took to be Adam and Eve in the garden, Noah and the animals, and other scenes from the bible as well. I caught my breath at the stunning beauty of it. I still cannot find the words to describe this room.

As in the first room, there were no windows and I did not see any type of lighting here, but again, it was well lit.

Suddenly, I felt uneasy as I stood there. I knew that I was not alone.

Shattering the serenity of this place, the room got very cold and I heard that same laughter that caused my skin to crawl. As I turned my head to look to see where the laughter had come from, I saw shadows on the top floor. As I looked closer, the carvings changed on the columns and became gargoyles. I saw the carved mouths move, and saw the eyes change from the polished wood to a fire red yellow color. They were alive! All around me the things of beauty were changing and becoming repulsive. My mind screamed, "NOT AGAIN, NOT HERE"!

In between the openings of the barriers, I saw glimpses of shadows running back and forth across the area on the top floor. I turned my body around to watch them, but they moved so fast, it was hard to keep up with where they were at the time. They were about two feet high and had horns on their heads. They were the shadow creatures that I had caught glimpses of earlier when the larger demons had arrived. They were not part of the large demons as they had been earlier and they keep running back and forth

Faith of a Child

across the area of the upper floor, but did not attempt to come to the lower floor. I don't know why, I didn't care at the time. I really didn't want to get that close to them again.

Just as suddenly as they started, they stopped and as I twisted my body around to look, they were gone and the place was as it had been when I walked in just a short time ago. I turned around to look at the center of the room again and saw to my surprised, a table that was about 4 feet high, with an angel standing behind it. He was holding a very large sword in both of his hands and the two men that I had been with earlier were standing on both ends of the table.

I walked over to the men and was about to ask a question when the first man pointed to my right and I saw two other angels standing off to one side of the room in an alcove of sorts, holding back a curtain that covered the entrance to a smaller room.

I walked over to that area of the room and passed thru the opening of the curtain and entered a small room, which was about 20 feet square. It had the same brick floor as the main room, and the walls were of the same white stone, but in the middle of this room, I saw what looked like a well or a deep water basin.

I was about to ask the angels what I was supposed to do here, but they had lowered the curtain back into place and I was alone.

I walked around in the room, trying to figure out what I was to do when I realized that this was an area for washing. The container the water was in was a little over two feet high and about six feet

Susan Lamar Blish

square, large enough to sit in. It was made of the same stone as the floor, but had no faucets that I could see and I imagined that the water came from a spring from below as the water kept moving. I wondered if perhaps it was a water baptism of sorts, but then I decided that it would not be possible, because a baptism was something that was usually done to you, not something that you would do yourself, and I was alone.

Before I disrobed, I walked around the basin and looked inside. I wondered if I was to actually get in the water or was I simply to use my hands to wash with. I noticed at the back, steps and decided that I was supposed to fully bath in this water. After disrobing, I placed my hand in the water and it was not hot or cold, but rather more of the same temperature as my skin and I almost didn't feel it. Slowly I climbed the stairs and lowered myself into the water. I had no sooner sat down and splashed water onto my face when I began to cry again. These tears however, were from a release deep within me. It was as if this simple task of bathing, was washing away all of the pain and tears that I had shed since my arrival. I lowered myself all the way into the bath and rinsed my hair as well and felt the freshness that comes from pure water. I splashed water onto my face again and finished washing away the tears and felt refreshed and renewed.

I slowly got out of the bath and dried myself using part of the robe that I had been wearing and once I was dressed, walked back in main room. I felt wonderfully clean after that bath. Really clean,

92

Faith of a Child

as if it had finished on the outside what God had started on the inside when He forgave me.

When I arrived back into the main room, I noticed upon the table, several objects that were not there when I had left. Now, there was a wooden cup, and a small loaf of what appeared to be bread.

As I approached the table, I saw that the wooden cup was holding some type of a liquid that was an amber color. The bread was all but flat, and it reminded me of pita bread that I usually get in the deli department of the grocery store.

I looked at the men then at the angel and then back at the men. The angel did not look at me, but continued to look straight ahead, never once lowering his sword.

I was not hungry and had no idea what these things were doing here and wondered if I was supposed to eat, but decided that if I was, the men would let me know. I felt a fragment of a memory from years ago, and then realized that this looked like a picture that I had seen once of a communion table.

"Is this was it was?" I asked myself, "A communion of sorts?"

I tried to remember a time in my life that I had partaken in a communion. In looking as far back as I could remember, I had never once been offered the chance to partake in a communion and honestly did not know what a communion was or what I or it was expected to do. Was this then, to be my first communion?

93

Susan Lamar Blish

I stood there fidgeting, not sure what I was supposed to be doing. Thankfully, it did not take long before the man with the book started to talk.

He opened his book and looked at me, his eyes piercing my soul and said "Precious child of The One True Living God, "The Ancient of Day's sent His son to walk amount you for a time so that you may live. When the Son was with you, He knew that He would soon be taken back to be with His father in heaven and wanted to assure His children of His return. His followers sat with Him and listened as He spoke saying to them:

"This is My body which is given for you, do this in remembrance of Me. This cup is the new covenant in My blood, which is shed for you."

The man looked at me, his eyes piercing my soul and said "Child of God, you must now decide for your self if you choose to partake of this communion. It is not a decision that should be entered into lightly. The message before you is this:

"Whoever eats the bread or drinks the cup of the Lord in an unworthy manner will be guilty of sinning against the body and blood of the Lord. A child of the Almighty God ought to examine themself before they eat of the bread and drink of the cup. For anyone who eats and drinks without recognizing the body of the Lord eats and drinks judgment on themself.

I stood there for several moments and my mind reeled with information and thoughts of every thing that I had experienced.

Faith of a Child

"Did I think I was worthy to finally do this?"

"Was this something that I really felt a need to do?"

"What were the reasons that a person would not partake?"

"Why would they?"

"Was I holding on to anything that would keep me from God at this point?"

"Was there any sin that I had not confesses or asked forgiveness for?"

"Was there a special blessing for me if I did?"

"What if I chose not to partake?"

"Did that mean that I didn't love God?"

"Was this one more test?"

With all of these thoughts in my mind, the man stood there holding his book open and waited and the man holding the scepter, looked at me his eyes narrowing.

After listening to the man, I walked off to one side of the room deep in thought and contemplation and then returned to the area where the men were still waiting, and stood quietly in my thoughts. I did not feel a pressure to make a decision, one way or the other. This I knew, was something that was very important and I wanted to be sure that I made the right decision. I knelt down and with no more thought of a decision than to ask God for guidance, something that I had not done before, I prayed. "Dear Father in Heaven, help me, your child, to know your will in my life in this decision. I do not want to offend you nor do I want to do something

Susan Lamar Blish

that is not required of me to do. I know Heavenly Father, that you will always be with me, and that you will never give me more than I am ready to handle, and I know too, that you will always give me a way out if you feel that I am not able to make those decisions. Thank you Father for your love and guidance and for the lessons you have allowed me to experience. Amen."

After I prayed, I stood quietly, looking at the table before me.

My eyes watered anew as I heard a sound slowly building. The choir of angels was back and I could hear their song, resonated through the temple. I had my decision.

"No", I told the man. "I can not partake of this communion. It is not that I do not feel worthy to partake of it, nor is it that in searching my self there is any reason that I can not partake of it, but I do not feel pressed by God to enjoy this. Perhaps in the future, He will press upon me and instruct me as to His desire, but at this time, it is not for me."

No sooner had I completed telling the men that I would not be taking the communion, when the tears started again. These were not tears of sorrow, these were tears of joy. I smiled through my tears as the angel's song built with such intensity that I felt it would lift me off my feet. I felt a bursting within me, and my body began to shake. I heard their song and saw a thousand colors crossed my eyes and I was shouting and praising God with every fiber of my soul! The Father, the Ancient of Day's, the one true and living God, had touched me and filled me with His spirit.

Faith of a Child

I stood there breathing in the scent of heaven and listened to the angels sing and shout. I was alive!

Soon, the temple became quiet again and I was left alone once again with the men. They did not show any emotion, they just stood there and looked at me. I just could not stop laughing and smiling. Never before in my life had I felt such a deep emotion and I honestly did not know if I would ever feel that again. To be filled with the Holy Spirit! It was such a thrilling and moving experience! I never wanted to loose that feeling and I knew that from this point forward in my life, I just needed to call on God and he would always answer me.

I sobered suddenly as the man with the scepter looked at me, his eyes narrowing. I took a step back from him as he raised his scepter in his one hand and with his other hand he pointed at me and shouted in a thunderous voice, "**CHALLENGE THEM!**"

Susan Lamar Blish

Chapter 10

…"Though I am surrounded by troubles, you

Will bring me safely through them. You will

Clench your fist against my angry enemies!

Your power will save me…"

(TLB Psalms 138:7)

Faith of a Child

THE CHALLENGE

As my mind was registering the words "Challenge them", I blinked and was back in the room with all of the other people.

I looked around for the mist but it was gone.

I had a feeling first of emptiness and then of uneasiness. All sound was muted and this was beginning to spook me. I franticly looked around for my mom and found her on my right. She too, was looking around as if trying to discern what had just happened.

The two men appeared once again and stood, not next to me as they had in the past, but rather, off to one side of the area I was standing in. I had no idea what I may have done if anything to upset them and cause them to stay away from me, but when I tried to walk to them, I found I was locked to my square of light. I did not like this; something told me that this was going be different from the things I had experienced in the past. I was right.

As I looked about me things began to change.

The light in the room changed and the area became dark. Not quiet as dark as midnight, but the same dark that you would see at twilight with that eerie color of black and white.

While I was standing there, I grabbed my mothers hand and pulled her to me. How she was able to leave her block of light was of no interest at the time. All I cared about was that she was standing next to me and we were together.

Susan Lamar Blish

I searched her face to see if she was aware of what we were going to have to do, but she just looked at me with tears streaming down her face. I was very surprised by this, as I can not remember the last time I had seen my mother cry, outside of this dream. It did not help with the unsettled feelings that I was having and I tried to comfort her.

As we were standing there trying to figure out what was going to happen, I heard a scream from some place off to my left. The mist was not in the room and I turned to see what would cause any one to scream when I saw them again. The demons were back! There were thousands of them! This time, they were not in the beautiful white, but remained as I had seen them before. When I saw them, a scream escaped from me as well. The room went cold and I felt that burn on my skin. I screamed again as something touched me. As I tried to brush it away, I heard that laughter again and a voice say; "He did leave you alone didn't he?" I yelled back "What do you want from me?"

All around the room, there was screaming and yelling. Panic was beginning to settle over the room as more and more people saw the demons or were touched by them.

Through my panic, I saw the demons move to each side of the area that I was on.

The man with the book was standing in front of me. How he had gotten there I have no idea, but it was the man with the scepter that

Faith of a Child

spoke this time. He raised his scepter into the air and in a thunder's voice said "All you need is faith in your God."

The floor, with no warning, suddenly separated into three tiers of equal length and width, much like a chess board. People were standing on each tier. The demons seemed to float up to what appeared to be a series of benches or bleachers set high off of the floor. I was standing on the top level. I knew I could see through the floor to the levels below me. The floor lit up in a series of lights, as if we were standing on pedestals of light.

It occurred to me that this was an arena of sorts!

The man with the book had not spoken yet and I looked at him wanting him to tell me what I was to do. He opened his book and read "The test consisted of the boxes of light and when they light up you *WILL* have to run to the next one that is lit and be on it to be protected from the demons."

He went on to say "the blocks of light will by your symbol standing for the light of God. As long as you are on one of the blocks of light, you will be safe from harm, for this is a safe zone. This is where God has allowed in this test that you will be protected from the demons." He went on to say "The point of the boxes and the lighting of them is your test of faith. Do YOU believe that God will get you to the next box? Do you doubt that He can carry you when you do not think you can make it? Will your fellow players help you or think only of themselves? Can you truly call on God when you need him and will he answer you and help you? Once

Susan Lamar Blish

you arrive on your block of light, you need to praise and worship God. And not just any praise or worship, but praise and worship truly and undeniably from your heart. If you do not praise in truth if you have DOUBT or you did not do it at the appropriate time with sincerity, the demons as well as God will see through that and the demons will in fact remove you from the game."

Once he had finished talking both men moved off to the side of the area I was standing on.

I looked around trying to understand what we had just been told; when I noticed that there were two classes of demons. Of the two the large one's, had floated up to the bleachers and were beginning to jeer and yell obscenities at us, and the others, the shadow one's, were separating from the larger ones, and were coming down to the area that we were standing on.

All of a sudden, some of the people in the room disappeared! I screamed "What's happening?!" The game as far as I knew, had not even started yet! I heard that laughter again. A voice said, "They didn't believe in God to start with, they can't play."

The floor went dark with no warning and I heard all around me people screaming and yelling. Suddenly the area that I was standing on got bright and I saw that the block in front of me was lit. I grabbed my mothers hand and yelled **RUN!** My mother in tow, I ran as fast as I could to the next block. No sooner had we arrived when the block two in front of us was lit and the one below my feet

Faith of a Child

went dark. I heard my mother praying and as I grabbed her arm again, ran to the next block all the while, praying "Lord save us!"

As I stood there, thanking God for getting me to this block of light, I saw the man on the row next to me suddenly stop! I screamed at him "RUN!" but he just looked at me and shook his head no and he stopped. The tears started again as the little demons were in our faces screeching at us and the noise from the larger demons was deafening.

I tried to push the little demons away when I saw that a new block was lit, but this one was five blocks in front of me. I started to run to it, the whole time praying that God would not leave me here. Not like this! I almost didn't make it to the block of light because my body began to hurt from the running. Just as I was beginning to wonder if I could make it, I heard one of the little demons screech at me, YOU CAN'T DO IT, YOU KNOW YOUR GOING TO FAIL, YOU ALWAYS DO!" It was with a new determination that I prayed and thanked God for this test. I bent over when I made it to the block of light from the pain of running. The tears would not stop, but I knew that I was safely with God.

The pattern on the floor changed and my row did not light up this time, but I watched others running back and forth. Some were almost to the next block of light and simply stopped. I, along with others yelled at them, RUN YOU CAN MAKE IT, but they just looked away and disappeared. More and more people were disappearing with each running. It was as if they had just given up!

103

Susan Lamar Blish

My mind was yelling NO, YOU CAN MAKE IT, but they didn't hear me and the little demons were yelling and screeching at them and it looked like they didn't care any more.

Suddenly my row was all lit and almost as a runway, some of the lights went out and I started to run again. This time, I was not allowed to slow down or stop fully, before the next block was lit and I had to run, and run, and run, and run, and run, back and forth from one end of the platform to the other. I don't know how long I ran but it took every ounce of strength that I had not to stop. The whole time I was running, I kept praying that God would get me to the next block of light. I told Him, "I know that I can not do this alone God, you have to help me." With each step that I took, I felt stronger in my faith. I knew without a doubt, that God would get me to the next block of light, and get me past this. I didn't think I would be able to run any more when there in front of me was a block of light, just a few blocks away, and all the rest were out. As I reached this block of light, my hands came up and my block of light became a small pedestal, rising slightly above the level of the floor.   ·

I stood there, and a new song formed in my mind. I began to sing this song with every ounce of faith and strength that I had. I stood there, singing this new song to God.

As I was standing there, once again I saw the mist. In it, I saw that I was in my apartment and finally made the decision to go to bed. When I arrived in the bedroom I discovered that only my small bedside light was on. I looked for and found every light in my room

Faith of a Child

was unplugged except for this one. I sighed as I plugged all of the others back in. With all of the lights on, I went to bed. I kicked off the blankets, and only had a light sheet covering me. With my head under a pillow, I tried to go to sleep while singing"this little light of mine, I'm going to let it shine." I heard the sound of that laughter again and felt the freezing burn that singles the demons were there. There was the sound of laughter and voices yelling and screaming; "YOU CAN'T DO IT, YOUR GOING TO FAIL, YOU ALWAYS DO!"

I cried again as I opened my eyes and saw that all of the lights were out in my room. The night lights, the overhead light in the closet all of them and it was pitch black in my room. I got out of bed and found that all of the lights had been unplugged. My tears came in rivers and the voices keep up the taunting.

Then, I heard a voice thunder "BE SILENCED!"

It was not a request. It was a COMMAND!

There was no sniffles, no whimpers, nothing. I looked around and saw the most brilliant light I have ever seen fill the room. This light was brighter than every sun you can imagine all at once filling this room.

That is when I discovered that the room was a deception, the walls were black, the bed linins were black, and the lights were not in fact as bright as I had thought.

I heard the voice tell me, "BE DECEIVED NO MORE" And I heard the choir of angels once again shouting Halleluiah!

105

Susan Lamar Blish

I knew that at last, as my heart filled with joy and the tears came from that joy, that Jesus was with me and that I would never again, walk alone, would never again have to fear the dark or what was in it. I was a child of The One True Living God, and nothing would ever shake my faith again.

The mist faded and I was back in the room, singing my song of praise to God when…

Far back in my mind, I heard something…..

Wake up! Ma'am, you need to wake up. Are you ok? What's wrong? Ma'am, wake up!

Faith of a Child

THE CHOICE

This story has been extremely hard for me to write. I had to face my entire life in a night and relive every thing that I had ever done, said, or thought.

I truly thank God that I had this chance and did not have to face the final judgment with all of this.

While I was dreaming, I learned a lot. Some things were very hard for me to face. I know that the truth can be painful, but not as much as the lies we tell ourselves and others.

The thing that saved me that night is the fact that God wants and desires to hear from us in truth and from our hearts and to know that we believe and trust in Him. This is of the utmost importance. He does not desire "lip service" or just the "show" that we are Christians. He wants and yearns for the proof of our faith, our belief and devotion to Him. When we are honest in our prayers, even with all the trappings that come with being "just human" He protects us from the demons of life and the pull they have on us. He will not forsake us or leave us if we are in fact "true in our hearts". And yet, because of the choice he gave us, if we are not honestly seeking His will in our life, He must allow us to "pay" for the choice that we have made and allow the demons to remove us for our lack of sincerity, our falseness to Him. And this causes him such pain that the tears he sheds for each of us hold all of our life in them.

107

Susan Lamar Blish

As I told my roommate about the dream, I began to understand the importance of the demons and the room. I was able to discover what had kept me from God. What I was doing in order not to have to face my own choices.

My head hurt with a new and severe clarity.

God had decided to show me the choice that I had made, and His desire for us thru his great love. When I went to bed that night in December, I thought I was a deeply devout Christian. I woke up knowing that I was wrong, so very wrong. There is so much more to being a Christian than just attending church services on Sunday morning. There is the asking for and accepting of Gods will in your life. There is the dedication of your life to the work He has for you. Then there is the actual work you must do. In changing your life and bringing it into full focus as a child of God, by allowing Him to work in you He will change you.

You need to put aside all of the trappings that come with not walking with God.

Some of the things that I have come to understand since that dream are the choices we make and the choices we allow others to make for us, so that we do not have to take responsibility for those actions or decisions. There is only one problem in that thinking. We WILL have to face those choices one day.

Each day, I face new choices in my life. Do I still stumble at times? Yes, but I know that God will forgive me. I know that all I need to do is ask and accept that forgiveness.

Faith of a Child

I work daily now on that change, to insure that when others see me, they see God in me and want to know the how's and why's of this change. Yes, I still get angry, I still hurt, I still make mistakes, and I am not perfect, only forgiven.

Knowing that we are children of God that he is always with us is in fact a small part of who we are, and what he desires us to be. We have for many years given into the desire of flesh. In truth God did not create us to forsake us. He created us to be with him.

If you are not sure you are doing all that your supposed to be doing, take a moment and think about every thing you have said, done or thought. Can you be sure that some one will not fall because of some action on your part? Can you be sure that God will accept your excuses if you were to stand before him this evening?

If you are not sure, then please take a moment and pray. Ask God to forgive you. Tell him that you are honestly sorry and that you know that you are lost and for a long time, did not think you could be forgiven. Then, accept His grace and forgiveness and believe that he forgives you and erased your past.

EPILOUGE:

The lord is my light and my salvation; whom shall I fear?

When evil men come to destroy me, they will stumble and

fall!

Yes, thought a mighty army marches against me, my

heart shall know no fear!

I am confident that God will save me.

(Psalms 27:1-3)

About the Author

Susan Lamar Blish was born in Tacoma, Washington and currently lives in University Place, Washington with her two cats, Rusty and Scampi.

She has three children—two boys and a girl—and seven grandchildren.

She has no professional training as a writer.

Her spare time is spent reading, doing needlepoint, and volunteering time at my church.

Printed in the United States
6366